Charles Arthur Kelly

Delhi and other Poems

Charles Arthur Kelly

Delhi and other Poems

ISBN/EAN: 9783337397678

Printed in Europe, USA, Canada, Australia, Japan

Cover: Foto ©Andreas Hilbeck / pixelio.de

More available books at **www.hansebooks.com**

D E L H I

AND OTHER POEMS

BY

CHARLES ARTHUR KELLY, M.A.

BENGAL CIVIL SERVICE.

NEW AND ENLARGED EDITION.

LONDON:

LONGMANS, GREEN, AND CO.

PATERNOSTER ROW.

1872.

PREFACE.

In SUBMITTING this little volume of collected
Poems to the judgment of those who may care
to honour them by a glance, I may perhaps be
allowed to mention that they were for the most
part written in India, in an atmosphere and
under conditions by no means congenial to effort
in the field of imagination. I am at the same
time well aware that I have no right to claim or
to expect any indulgence either from the critic
or the reader on that account.

The present edition comprises, in addition to

' Delhi and other Poems' and ' The World's Martyrs ' (originally published separately in India), some pieces hitherto unpublished, and some which have previously appeared in the ' Calcutta Review ' and ' Englishman.'

C. A. KELLY.

CONTENTS.

CONTENTS.

Errata

Page 114, line 1, stanza 2, *for* never *read* ever

„ 148 „ 5, *for* illumines *read* illumes

PRELUDE.

I READ those bright Italian lays that sound
Wild as the lark's song—wild—but passing sweet,
While showered the rose-leaves, till the glad green
    ground
  Grew red beneath my feet.

Till their deep music melted into tears
My heart, weighed down with silent sense of wrong,
As one by one the glories of past years
  Flashed from the chords of song.

I felt a mighty impulse heave and swell
Within me, but a still voice rang out clear,
As floats the full tone of a grand church bell
  O'er storm-swept waters drear.

B

'Ah, well,' I sang, 'those lofty minstrel souls
Work the full purpose of their faith in me,
They knew the power that conquers and controls
  With subtlest harmony,

They knew that though their white Italian graves
Lie cypress-shrouded underneath the blue,
Yet their strong will should beat, while beat the
    waves,
  In noble hearts and true.

High souls soar ever high, for weal or woe,
They cannot rest, they move, they meet their fate,
They hear a voice that summons them to go,
  And warns them to be great.

Some, after death, we shun as meteor lights
On the dark ground where common mortals grope,
Some, through the utter darkness of our nights,
  Hurl the bright shafts of hope.

Sleep on, young dreamer, with the cold white brow,
Pure as thine own poetic love divine,
Out-welling passionate prayer and breathless vow,
   Thy lady's name the shrine.

Sleep on, but if perchance a passing dream
Of past days haunt the still rest of the tomb,
If once again thy golden fancies stream
   Through murmurous depths of gloom,

Then thy winged thoughts awakened shall return,
And quick warm life shall stir the death-chilled
    dust,
And thy loved Laura's gentle eyes shall burn,
   Bright in their own calm trust.

And ye shall wander far beyond the stars,
Drink the pure truths by perished ages taught
From those glad founts no mortal weakness bars,
   Untraversed realms of thought.

Though Petrarch was a being of this earth,
Yet songs that burn, and strains that will not die,
Bear in themselves, as earnest of their birth,
   An immortality.

And doth not that creative Bard rest well,
Though storm-winds rave through shuddering pines
     above,
Calm as the lone sea-deeps, whose heart could tell
   The Hundred Tales of Love ?

What though for eyes as bright, and brows as fair,
Still breathes the minstrel, and still sounds the lute,
Weep, for Boccaccio's spirit is not there,
   The master lyre is mute.

O that *my* lips could utter words of fire,
The secret voice within me peal aloud,
But aye soar upward, as the gray church-spire,
In sunshine and in cloud.

For well I know that over all the God
Sits brooding, and our best rays are but dim,
Towards one great Light all earthly paths are trod,
   And all shall end in Him.

He hath not known the stirring truths of life,
Who dreams and muses till the day's gone by,
He only feels, who battles in the strife,
   A glad futurity.

DELHI.

Canto I.—THE EMPIRE.

From that far clime where buried empires sleep,
There floats a mighty voice that makes me weep.
Ah, voice of woe! what mortal tongue may tell
How rose the ancient thrones, and how they fell!

A visioned splendour of a vanished fate,
A city crowned with more than mortal state.
There in old years the royal banquet glowed,
From minstrels' lips the melting numbers flowed;
Voluptuous strains the despot's heart beguiled,
And blushing beauties trembled as they smiled.
Well might they fear a Lord, whose lightest breath
Could change their songs of joy to shrieks of death.

Then round their chief, like storm-clouds round a
    star,
The swift Mahratta squadrons rushed to war,
With one wild yell their myriads rose in might,
And neighed the war-horse frantic for the fight.

Then the stern Saxon from a stranger land,
Fire in his eyes, and conquest in his hand.
Weep for the glorious dead by whom were wrought
Those feats of war, those master-works of thought.
Mourn for the men of might—how few survive
Who rule like Hastings, or who fight like Clive !

No more, but let me wander by the stream,
Where Delhi rises on me like a dream,
There let my spirit trace the golden thread
That winds from silent chambers of the dead,
And drink a deep delight, while Fancy flings
Her sunny robe o'er shrouded queens and kings.

Such themes, with burning passion born of pain,

I've loved, and trust I have not loved in vain,

For thoughts of vanished glory charm the grief

Of this cold age, and yield a sad relief.

Where a great river rolls through cypress shades,

Death-smitten streets, and desolate colonnades—

For Time and War their blasting brand have set

On saintly mosque and sparkling minaret—

By glad waves kissed, and lulled in murmurs deep,

My city laughs her loveliness to sleep.

Seek not from pictured urn or storied bust

When first imperial Delhi woke from dust,[1]

Long ere the royal city rose in state,

Assumed an empire, and fulfilled her fate,

And o'er her birth the mist of ages throws

Majestic gloom, and motionless repose.

[1] The origin of ancient Delhi is shrouded in obscurity.

Then,   borne   on   eagle   wings,   she   burst   from
    night,

Shook off the chain of years, and soared to light.

Full many a bard has sung with heart of fire

Her pride of place, the glories of her lyre;

In saddening strains full many a harp recalls

Her long array of triumphs and of falls.

Sound the wild war-note over Eastern fields,

And chant the dirge of death, for Delhi yields!

The potent slave,[1] Mohammed's favourite, comes,

With stately march, and thundering roll of drums !

Yet many a shock of war the city stood,

Till her own Jumna's loving waves ran blood,

And with stern heart, and swift pursuing spear,

Rushed on the foe the Rajpoot mountaineer.

So fought the brave of old, but fought in vain ;

The vanquished pine beneath the Gaurian chain.

---

[1] Kootub-ood-deen Eibuk.

Yet the young empire wrought her high renown,

What time the Gaurian Moslem held the crown ;

O'er many a field her conquering banner flew,

And myriads trembled when the sword she drew.

Proud in her might, she laughed her foes to scorn,

And grew in splendour like the rising morn,

Nor dreamed of future years, when thundering loud

Burst on her head the destined battle-cloud.

She falls—nor may her towers of strength disdain

The scourge of God, the conquering Tamerlane.

Lo, the fierce Tartar o'er the shaking land

Sweeps like a fire from sunlit Samarcand,

His blood-red footsteps hailed by dying groans,

Lost fights, and monarchs trembling on their thrones.

' In Delhian vaults lie wealth of ancient gems,

Store of red gold, and dazzling diadems ;

Such princely spoils our warrior hearts shall cheer,

A glittering guerdon for the Mogul spear.'

I see the vengeful spearmen throng the street;

I hear the savage shout, the tramp of feet;

Shrill clanged the cruel steel, the midnight air

Froze with the shriek of horror and despair;

Babes from their shuddering mother's breasts were
    torn,

And, red from midnight horrors, blushed the morn.

Then left the sullen foe the place of doom,

As sweeps from wasted lands the spent simoom,

While the sad city swooned before their breath,

Like some fair princess stricken near to death.

Again the Mogul battle-flags, unfurled

For death or victory, challenge half the world;

On Eastern gales the Tartar clarions sound,

And mounted myriads lightly hover round.

Why press with furious haste the marshalled powers,

And spur their steeds on Delhi's kingly towers?

Why on their leader's forehead lowers a gloom
Shall burst in thunder ?   'Tis the day of doom.

Day breaks, but ere yon glorious sun sinks down,
Two rival hosts shall battle for a crown.[1]
Rings on the breeze the Afghan's laugh of scorn,
And shrill the Tartar war-cry wakes the morn.
Well may the Mogul view with glance of light
His eager troopers rouse them for the fight,
The Delhian despot tremble in his pride,
And half betray the fear he strives to hide.
Then one wild rush (as sweep the drifted snows
Down dark ravine), and hand-to-hand they close.
Swift on the serried ranks the Delhians dash,
As leaps upon the rock the lightning-flash,
While the stern Tartar, griping fast the spear,
Hails each wild onset with a wilder cheer.

[1] The Afghan dynasty of Lodi was overthrown by the victory
of the Mogul Baber on the plain of Paniput (so often the theatre
of great battles) on April 21, 1526.   Ibrahim Lodi, king of
Delhi, was killed during the fight.

Fierce flames the strife, the blood-drops fall like rain,

And the dread tramp of warriors shakes the plain.

All day the battle raged with equal might,

As when two storm-clouds meet on mountain height.

Unscathed all day the Delhian banner flew,

At fall of night the Mogul overthrew.

Then the wild rout of horror and of fear,

The fiery Tartar hurrying on the rear,

The fallen war-horse, and the shivered spear.

Sound a lament! and let the mournful strain

Breathe peace to Delhian hearts and soothe their pain;

For many a warrior noble, many a chief,

Lie cold on yonder field of death and grief.

Let Delhi weep her shattered strength, and fling

A royal death-shroud o'er her vanquished king.

I hear the conquerors shout, the vanquished groan,

'Allah Akbar, the Mogul's on the throne!'

The day of gloom has past, I see the star
Of brightening Eastern glory glance afar.

'Twas then the wondrous empire first had birth,
The sceptred sway that soared too high for earth,
Then Delhi sat on high, while fire and sword
Made myriads own the Mogul for their lord,
Saw her imperial might supreme confest,
Then, wrapt in dreamy splendour, sank to rest;
Unmoved, saw monarchs fall and nations weep,
A proud Sultana lulled in sensual sleep;
While the far East upon her lap unrolled
All sparkling spoils of purple and of gold,
And minstrels sang, 'The light of other lands
May sink in endless gloom, but Delhi stands !
All other empires Time and War shall blight,
Or hurl them headlong from their giddy height,
But she shall view their fall with front serene,
For ever fair, the world's Eternal queen ! '

She longed for lordly towers to soar sublime

In massive splendour, sparkling as her clime,

And bade her builders trace the lofty line,

And clothe in clear-cut stone the rare design,

Wherein her royal soul might rest at ease,

Nor languish for far lands, and unknown seas.

With cunning hand those ancient workmen wrought

The grand creations of poetic thought;

Like some sweet vision grew the glorious shade,

The solemn arch, the stately colonnade ;

Rose saintly minaret and splendid dome,

And in wreathed silver laughed the fountain foam.

Who loves to muse on glory sunk in gloom,

May view Death's royal house, Humayoon's tomb,

Meet for a Mogul emperor's buried state,

Even in his last repose magnificently great.

Then we may heavenward cast our eyes and scan

Yon Gothic mosque,[1] that glorious work of man.

[1] The Jumna Musjid.

There when the Day God delicately frets
With virgin gold the bright twin minarets,
The Muezzin's shrill tones pierce the startled air,
' Allah Akbar! Mohammed's sons, to prayer!'
Well may the white-robed votaries gather round,
And deem the courts they tread are holy ground,
For ne'er, since Islam's conquering creed had
    birth,
Boasts her false prophet nobler shrine on earth,
Than where yon Eastern temple towers sublime,
And splendid Superstition laughs at time.

And lo! the vast and crowning work of might,
The Hall of Kings and palace of delight!
Time hath not changed, nor wasting war subdued
Yon dome divine, or bright wall sunset-hued;
Nor dimmed the varied tints, the living glow
Of rose-red sandstone dashed by marble snow.
Behold the kingly arch that spans the gate,
Bright as Heaven's glorious bow, and fixed as fate.

Stern frowns the tower of strength, but free and far,

High o'er the massive roof each light minar

Soars toward the clouds, and sparkles like a star.

Or view with awe-struck eyes the wondrous aisle,

When streams the moonlight like an angel's smile.

There lives in stone the artist's rare design,

Green leaves, fair flowers, and sculptured texts divine.

Wrought to the life, the pictured bulbul sings,

And the limned tiger crouches ere he springs,

Blooms the blue lotus delicately clear,

And blush the breathing roses of Cashmere.

Then leave the Hall of State, and wander far

Thro' the green glades of silent Shalamar,

Where foamed in ancient days the swift cascade,*

And o'er bright lamps the mimic rainbow played.

---

[1] 'The gardens, which are extensive, and were formerly adorned with fountains, miniature cascades, so constructed that the sheet of water fell over a number of lamps placed in recesses in the wall behind, &c.'—*Handbook of Delhi.*

Love the deserted groves, for ever mute,
Mourn the dead minstrel, the forgotten lute.

In yon imperial halls they lay reclined,
Those lords of earth, and monarchs of mankind :
Around me breathe the love, the hate, the fears,
The thousand passions of those burning years :
When ruled the wise in council, great in war,
And just in heart, magnificent Akbar ;
When Selim's love bade empires rise or fall
To charm the wayward heart of Nourmahal ;
When the arch-traitor, Aurungzebe, arose,
And with wild war-notes scared his sire's repose,
Saw one by one his baffled foes fall down,
And staked his lying soul to win the crown.

They lived, and loved, and died, and left a name
Writ in blood-letters on the page of Fame.
From Baber, builder of the lofty rhyme,
The warrior poet of the olden time,

Down to a gray old man, an exiled slave,
A crownless monarch, and a nameless grave.

Theirs the wild joy that Orient despots know,
Blue skies above, and glowing earth below.
'Twas theirs to rouse the princely chase, and scare
The monarch of the jungle from his lair.
In all the glittering pomp of Eastern pride,
Around their king the jewelled nobles ride;
All day they tracked the monster's sullen flight,
Till fled the tropic day from dewy night.
Then in the royal tent the feast was spread,
Fair shone the moon, and streaming over head,
The Delhian flag in many an ample fold
Flung to the breeze its blazoned waves of gold.

Ah happy nights! when Venus' lonely star
Rose o'er the groves of cypressed Shalamar;
Then the gay court on flowery slopes reclined,
Gave care and sorrow to the fanning wind,

And black-eyed houries mingled in the dance,

Bright as the flashing flies that o'er them glance,

(Bring gems to bind on their thin-veinèd wrist,

Bring snowy pearl, and tender amethyst,)

Or soft strains woke beneath the minstrel's hand,

As of an exile mourning for his land.

Hail to the magic harp! that pierced **the** throng

With melancholy joy, when thus the **song,**

After a passionate prelude, made its way,

Scarce heard above the foam-fount's dashing spray.

'With sunlight crowned, and flushed with pomp of
    war,

O'er Eastern waves the land I love lies far.

There evermore the south wind, breathing balm,

Sighs a sweet song thro' feathery groves of palm,

Nor nature's voice alone, for evermore

Our girls' glad laughter rings from shore to shore.

Ah well-beloved! whene'er our steps roam forth

From thy fair clime, and faithless seek the North,

We feel as though we had wandered far away,
To realms of night from regions of the day,
We yearn for light, we rest not till we feast
Our longing eyes on thee, thou glorious East!'

What warrior comes? what chieftain leads the van
From the sung streets of storied Isfahan?
Let vanquished myriads waft his fame afar,
The Persian chief, the shepherd Lord of War,
What empire knows not Nadir's ruthless hand?
Let Delhi tremble when she draws the brand!

Throw wide the royal gates to entertain
Those awful guests, the Persian and his train;
To you stern despot bow with homage meet,
And throw thy golden treasure at his feet.
He comes, the stranger, doomed to change ere long
Battle's loud chorus for the banquet-song,
For festive hall, the chamber of the dead,
For sparkling wine, War's deep draught bloody-red.

Hears not the Tyrant, while he sits in state,

The rushing wings of an avenging fate,

The clang of thirsty steel, the gasping breath

Of those stern souls that only yield to death,

And shrieks, and sobs, and lamentations wild,

As of a mother mourning for her child?

Yet his red hand the slaughter will not stay

Till Rage and Hate have foamed themselves away;

Then all is hushed, and Delhi mourns alone,

Reft of her crown, her jewels, and her throne.

Why task the minstrel's sorrowing heart to tell

How year by year the ancient empire fell,

As some fair Lady yields to slow decay,

And smiles her dying loveliness away.

More shapes of woe the future years shall bring,

A ghost of state, a phantom of a King,

I see a Prince, a blind old man, bow down,

Shame for his robe and ruin for his crown,

And trembling tones, that thrilled o'erwhile with grief,

Breathe a glad welcome to an English chief.[1]

Of ancient Delhian glories what remain ?

Seven leagues of ruin on an Eastern plain.

Where round yon mouldering tower the dank weeds

    cling,

And the grim vulture wheels on phantom wing,

There erst the Delhian minstrel tuned his lute,

And sang the charms of ladies, long since mute.

Yon shattered steps the splendid despot trod,

Whom servile millions worshipped as a god.

There's not a stone of yon gray mosque but bears

Some stirring memory of long vanished years,

When fast and far the Imperial eagles soared,

And vanquished India found a Delhian lord.

Where now those men of might, thus cold in dust,

Their pomp, their pride, their glory, and their trust!

[1] An allusion to Lord Lake's entry into Delhi in 1803. The
unhappy emperor of that day had been blinded some years previously by the Rohilla chief, Gholám Khadir.

Well may we pause, and pray with tears of pain,

We may not read this awful page in vain,

Nor wish for buried kings, or chieftains brave,

More proud memorial, or a grander grave.

Canto II.—THE MUTINY.

Still, as of old, the glancing fountains play,
Thro' the long sunshine of the tropic day.
Still, faint with death, the odorous night-breeze
    waves
The palms that cluster round our warriors' graves;
Still, flashing thro' the gloom, the firefly's light
With twinkling diamonds decks the brow of night;
Still Jumna whirls his glittering power along,
The theme of many an Eastern poet's song;
Still, the loved brighteners of that poet's dream,
Thro' deep green leaf the snow-white minarets gleam;
But ah! how fallen from her ancient worth,
Delhi, the great, the Elysium of the earth!
Yet to speak lightly of her name beware;
To fade is but the fate of all things fair.

Alas, thrice conquered city ! thou hast felt

The fall of pride.   When monarchs round thee knelt,

When thou wast hailed Eternal, when the might

Of thy dread sons, victorious in the fight,

Swept onward o'er the bounds of utmost Ind,

Like a strong storm-cloud driven by the wind,

Did some high bard, thrilled with prophetic fire,

To melancholy chords attune his lyre,

Did he foretell, when yet thy sovereign Fate

Seemed thro' all time imperishably great,

How Clive should lead his warriors from afar,

Armed with dread thunders from the Western star,

Flushed with the fame of Plassey's deathless field,

And in one day bid a whole empire yield ?

How, in the future ages of the world,

A mighty wrath against thy greatness hurled,

Should lay thee low in dust, while o'er thy head

The blue-eyed Saxon's hated race should tread ?

When death's shrill tones should break thy dreamy

    rest,

And war's red waves rush foaming from the West ?

In those far times old Delhi sat in power,

Queen of the East, the wealth of Ind her dower.

What are her triumphs, what her glories now ?

A withered laurel on a recreant brow ;

For those dark murders done by Jumna's shore

Shall haunt her towers till time shall be no more !

O for a Byron's fire, a Milton's might,

To wail our woes in words of living light ;

To chant the death-dirge for their souls, who fell

By Delhi's marble palaces of hell ;

Where England's mothers (hear it, England !) kneel,

But find no mercy save the accursed steel ;

Where children's wailings load the tainted air,

And angels shudder at the old man's prayer.

Weep for the golden tresses steeped in blood,

Weep for the woes of England's womanhood,

Weep for our murdered infants' stifled cry,

Weep for the strong man's silent agony,

Weep for the loved ones early doomed to part,

Weep for the anguish of the pure in heart!

For fairer suppliants never bowed the head,

Since Rachel's tears would not be comforted;

And slaves more bloody never drew the brand,

Since Herod's vengeance cursed his red right hand!

The fair child lying, half her bosom bare,

Half buried in a depth of golden hair,

All deadly white, but with a deadlier glow,

A bubbling crimson dyes the cold chaste snow.

No more those eyes, lit up with lustrous gleam,

Glance like the star's light on a storm-tost stream,

No more the young soul lends the young lips breath,

Lovely in life, but more divine in death.

God rest her, calm in dust! but who shall say

How many a heart is broken far away!

How many an old man feels the hot tears start

For her he loved, the darling of his heart!

Slight griefs may stir the fount of tender years,

But awful import dwells in old men's tears :

They breathe the shattered sense, the mindless rave,

Grey hairs brought down with sorrow to the grave.

On Eastern shores the far-off surges sweep,

In English homes the widowed mourners weep.

When dies the daylight, and the wind wails high,

How many an angel face looks toward the sky,

Lit with a melancholy light divine,

Like a saint's statue in a ruined shrine.

Heaven knows the rest—no mortal eyes intrude

Into the calm of that deep solitude.

Yet mourn them not as lost, our sons that lie

In lonely rest beneath an Indian sky ;

Let faith and hope be mingled while ye weep,

' For so He giveth his beloved sleep,'

Where, safe from murderers' hands and war's alarms,

They slumber in the everlasting arms.

Yettremble ! for the shaft of Fate has sped ,

Tremble, ye slavish souls, ye worse than dead !

Warrers on women, tremble ! there has rung

The cry of 'War' from every English tongue ;

And England's wrath is hurrying o'er the deep,

For her great sorrow will not let her sleep.

Lo ! her great war-fleet hears her high behest,

Charged with the vengeful terrors of the West,

Tossed by the mighty ocean's foaming breath,

Swift as the storm, and winged as sleepless death.

Now Western warriors throng the Eastern strand,

And clanging horsehoofs echo through the land,

'Onward for Delhi ! let the guilty feel

The keen stern temper of our Saxon steel !

Onward for Delhi ! pluck the regal crown

From her high head, and hew the oppressor down.

Woe to the scornful city's impious pride,

Woe to the lips that mocked when children died !

Not long unheard shall India's thirsty sod,

Red with the blood of patriots, call to God ;

Not long their bones shall whiten on the plain ;
For England draws the sword, nor draws in vain.'

Again thy mournful light shall shine full soon
On scenes of war, thou glorious Eastern moon ;
Full soon shall Delhi wake from sinful sleep,
When round her walls the avenging army sweep.

'Tis well, that on our camp the grim guns frown,
The Delhian strongholds on our host look down ;
Our bosoms throb with rapture, stern but deep,
For holy watch and ward 'tis ours to keep.
'Tis thus, with swords unsheathed, and white tents
    spread,
We Christian warriors come to mourn our dead !

'Twere long to tell, how many a weary day
By Delhi's blood-stained walls the avengers lay ;
How some, that sought to rescue, found a grave ;
How boomed the cannon, and how fought the brave ;

How hearts, too great to murmur, throbbed with
    grief,
What time Death's angel bore away their chief.
Desperate the chance : they die, or win the walls ;
No hope for England's sons till Delhi falls !

With brand up-raised, and white plume flashing far,
What haughty chieftain holds the front of war ?
Well knows the foe that warrior in the fight,
Stern as the storm, and terrible as night ;
Not his to dread the battle's blood-red waves,
Nor the wild rush of Heaven-detested slaves,
Though from the thundering bastion bursts the cloud,
And the thick war-smoke clothes him like a shroud.
On towards the gate of Death he pressed, and fell,
The proud stern man they feared, yet loved so well ;
Quenched by the death-shot, lie for ever still
That iron spirit and that master will,
The princely heart of steel that would not yield,
But, like the Spartan, died upon the shield.

Say not such earnest toils were borne in vain ;

Who wins the glory first must feel the pain.

Champion of right, the noblest aim of man,

He lived, and died when vengeance led the van.

May loftier harps record his glorious youth,

His love of honour, and his living truth,

We only mourn for him whose work is done,

And wish the world had more like Nicholson !

'No time for fruitless tears! who heads the attack ?

Life, if we win ; Death, if we are driven back.

Think on the widow's shriek, the orphan's tears,

And that great fame we won in ancient years,

The fair-haired girls that mourn, the babes that weep,

O manly hearts, be stedfast, and strike deep !

So shall ye tread the path your fathers trod,

True to yourselves, your country, and your God,

Though angry Death hurl bullets thick as hail

From his red hand, and ride upon the gale.

We cherish with a pure and holy pride

The houschold-loves for which our fathers died :

Dear are our daughters, dear the calm delight

Of girls' eyes beaming round our hearths at night,

And dear the memory of young tears that flow,

The voiceless soothers of our hours of woe.

The hand that dared with Death's dark stream to dye

The inner veil of virgin purity,

Has touched a quivering chord that will not rest,

And stirred the inmost fountains of the breast.

Not long shall Delhi's towers exulting stand,

To-morrow's light we storm them sword-in-hand,

And our great wrath to all the world shall tell

That England loves her murdered children well ! '

Hark to the shout of hosts, where Jumna's wave

Chants a wild requiem for the good and brave !

The red light flashes through the eddying smoke,

And swords glance upward as the lines are broke,

Ne'er ebbed the tide of war since Time began,

When England's Lion banner leads the van.

As the lone eagle, nursed on heights of snow,

Burns with a fire unknown to realms below,

So the hot valour, born of English air,

Spurs on our Saxon hearts to do and dare.

Attest it, Flodden! when the dauntless ring

Stood, wrapt in glooms of death, around their king.

Attest it, ye who saw what deeds were done,

When in close fight the well-stormed gate was won.

Mourn, Delhi, mourn! thy vanquishéd sons have fled,

And thou art but the Empress of the dead.

Gone is thy high renown of other days,

Thy barbarous grandeur sung in ancient lays.

For England plants her standard on thy walls,

And Christians throng thy sacred temple halls.

Let the proud song of triumph spread like flame,

And righteous justice track the deed of shame;

Let outraged Albion find an exile's grave
For the last Mogul, far beyond the wave.

Though Havelock slumbers on a foreign shore,
His lifelong toils and deathless conquests o'er,
Though England mourns with more than Roman
    grief
The far-off grave of many a victor chief,
Though many a hero's bright blue eyes are dimmed,
For many a soul the funeral-dirge is hymned,
And many a mother weeps till drearier dawn
Breaks the dead night, from all, save God, withdrawn,
Yet shall they say, proud smiling thro' their tears,
' He sleeps, full old in fame, though young in years.
His grave is with the mighty ones who fell
Hushed in that iron storm of shot and shell,
On that red field where England's valour shone,
Bright as the Athenian fire at Marathon,
Where the loud death shriek, thrilling thro' the sky,
Fired the proud soul, and made the heart beat high,

Where England's sons 'gainst traitor hosts arrayed,

For Eastern empire drew the avenging blade,

Where rebel India felt the hand of Fate,

And Freedom smiled serene by Delhi's shattered

    gate.'

THE WORLD'S MARTYRS.

Faith alone can interpret life, and the heart that aches and
    bleeds with the stigma
Of pain, alone bears the likeness of Christ, and can comprehend
    its dark enigma.
LONGFELLOW's Golden Legend.

Now, when the winds of autumn, piping loud,

Arise, and chant the death-dirge of the year,

Faint spirit voices call me from the crowd,

    I cannot choose but hear.

Through every chord of grief those voices range,

In melancholy music, soft and low,

They tell of years that long have suffered change,

    Of ages long ago.

Sometimes, moreover, a great victor-shout,

As warriors raise upon the battle-day,

Far o'er the tenderer tones of woe rings out,

    And slowly dies away.

A mighty chant of woes, and wars, and wrongs,

That haunts me with a wild and weird-like spell,

Sorrow and joy are mingled in their songs,

    And love unspeakable.

   .   .   .   .   .   .

A mountain church-yard, where through gloom pro-

        found,

The sad cold tombstones glimmer ghastly white,

And the great waves majestically sound

    A requiem, day and night.

Thither, when faithless swallows leave the North,

And Earth's dark paths with sweet gold leaves are

        spread,

At fall of night I love to wander forth,

    And muse upon the dead.

And night has come.   Among a thousand stars,

Swift sails the white moon through the sapphire

       blue,

Like a fair Queen, who leads to glorious wars

  Her steel-robed warriors true.

' Break into foam, O bright and boundless sea,

Sleepily hurl thy waters evermore !

So float the calm tides of Eternity

  Upon the golden shore.

So o'er our dull souls, lost in sensual sleep,

The glimpses of the glory come and go,

So fall the large pearl-tears that angels weep,

  On the dark world below.

As on the unfeeling sands thy solemn waves

Dash idly, so upon the shores of Fate

Rolls the deep voice, that thunders from the graves

  Of the departed great.

Yes, they have past into the golden age ;

Far from this weary world in peace they lie ;

And who are we should grasp their heritage

    Of thoughts that may not die ?

Also the snowy statues delicate,

And pictures ever-burning from the walls,

Where Art, eternal and serene as Fate,

    Smiles in her thousand halls.

This cry breaks on me from the world's chill gloom,

' What care we for the glorious names of old ?

Let Genius sleep forgotten in the tomb,

    So we may grasp the gold.'

Only the everlasting stars above

Gaze down upon their graves in holy trust,

Only the cypress, with eternal love,

    Droops o'er their sacred dust.

So mused I, sorrowing, while the moon-lit yews
Shook their broad arms in grand responsive grief,
Then all was calm, while tear-like glanced the dews
   On each funereal leaf.

But on my ears a strange sweet melody
Came blended with a solemn rush of wings,
As when in full and awful symphony
   An angel sweeps the strings.

And then I knew that I was not alone ;
Two queen-like shapes were standing by my side ;
Far-glancing through the gloom their faces shone
   With light love-sanctified.

One robed in spotless white, no sparkling gems
Marred the soft lustre of her eyes' calm glow,
But, more august than regal diadems,
   The laurel wreathed her brow.

The other's night-black garments swept the ground,
The ever-mourning cypress clasped her head,
With lustrous tears her full large orbs were drowned,—
　　Tears such as martyrs shed.

They sang to me upon the mountain's crown,
Never was earth-born music half so fair
As those sweet strains, that soft and cold fell down,
　　Like snow-flakes through the air.

' Thou, whose sad tones of natural human woe
Have touched us, watching on the eternal shore,
Follow thou us, and following thou shalt know
　　To weep again no more.

' We are the guardians of the world's true kings ;
Glory and Anguish are our names, well known
To those who, after thousand sufferings,
　　Rest by the golden throne.

' 'Tis we who soothe the Patriot's dying pains,
Who, smote when battling in the foremost place,
Sheds his last life-blood on his country's plains,
   A smile upon his face.

' Whene'er the Poet lifts his voice of fire,
Hurling his war-shafts 'gainst a giant wrong,
'Tis we who prompt the utterance of his lyre,
   And nerve his deathless song.

' Thus work we out God's ancient purpose high,
As stedfast and unwearying as the sun,
And Time shall yield to vast Eternity,
   Before our work be done.

'Ah, not for nought the sympathy sublime
Of those great human drops of blood that He,
The Lord of every age and every clime,
   Shed in Gethsemane.

'And not for nought the burden and the heat,
Borne by those few but chosen souls, who know
That there is nothing on this earth so sweet,
　　As high heroic woe ! '

They ceased.　I knew no language for reply,
But as, where Arctic billows heave and roll,
The great lights shoot across the dreary sky,
　　That broods around the pole,—

So this strange music flashed into my blood,
And smote me with the love of glorious pain,
And lofty thoughts came surging like a flood,
　　And rushed through heart and brain.

And then, while on my temples leapt a flush,
And in quick heart-beats throbbed my burning breath,
' Led by such glorious guides, 'twere sweet to rush
　　Into the arms of Death ! '

Thus, in the tumult of a wild delight,

I spoke—then came a solemn pause of dread,

While those two Sovereign Sisters, prompt for flight,

    Their stately wings outspread.

Her of the snowy robes I followed fast

Through the thick darkness, many and many a rood,

Until we came into a forest vast,

    An awful solitude.

Wherein no gladsome trees or wild flowers sprung,

Only the dark yew and the cypress frowned,

And giant oaks their spectral arms outflung

    Over the desolate ground.

And through the shades a sullen river hurled

Deep night-black waters, grimly murmuring,

Like that famed Lethe of the lower world,

    Whereof old Poets sing.

Then I, as one who hears the trumpet call,

And knows that he is hastening to his tomb,

Yet, nerved for one great war-deed e'er he fall,

    Goes forth to meet his doom.

Thus, though deep gloom my senses overbore,

Freezing my blood, I trod each devious glade,

And intricate dark wood-walk, evermore

    Clothed in a deeper shade.

A palpable gross darkness overhead,

Nor any happy glimpse of sun or moon,

The solemn groves lay leagues on leagues outspread,

    Sunk in a death-like swoon.

At last a choral anthem, full and soft,

Came faintly floating towards us on the gale,

Whereof the glorious burden soared aloft,

    ' O victor-souls, all hail! '

And I grew glad, for this proud Pæan thrilled

My heart, as sun-parched flowers the summer rains,

And my quick blood, so numbed erewhile and chilled,

    Ran pulsing through my veins.

And then, as one who marks at early dawn

The glorious eastern sun arise in might,

I saw the dreary veil of gloom withdrawn,

    Shot through with shafts of light.

And full in front a massive Temple fair,

Royally built, shone queen-like in the glow

Of delicate veined marble, rich and rare,

    White as the drifted snow.

I heard the deep-toned voice of mighty choirs,

From hidden nave and transept rising high;

I saw ten thousand pinnacles and spires

    Soar sparkling to the sky.

Soul-struck I hurried on—I could not wait—
The strong-winged angels rushing still before,
I passed within the massive golden gate
    Unto a crystal floor.

Where, wreath on wreath, rich clouds of incense smoke
From silver censers rising, filled the air—
Chased by a million rose-hued rays that broke
    Through blazoned windows rare.

Then all my blood rushed upward in a glow,
For, through the rolling smoke clouds dimly seen,
Faint spirit-shapes were fleeting to and fro
    Of most majestic mien.

The Statesman, with his proud stern lips compressed,
As when the keen debater's arrowy scorn
Flashed on him, calm, as claiming to be blessed
    By ages yet unborn.

The Poet, with an upturned face of awe ;
Musing he seemed on angel-haunted skies,
But trembling, for the glory that he saw
  Shot frenzy through his eyes.

The Painter, like a god's his large white brow,
Of holiest thoughts the holy marble shrine,
His clear-cut earnest features all a-glow
  With dreams of shapes divine.

And lovely ladies met in radiant bands,
Holding sweet earnest converse, each with each,
I saw the glimmer of their snowy hands,
  I heard their silver speech.

But their fair faces, indistinct and faint,
Glanced to and fro in many a mystic gleam,
Like those calm anguished eyes of virgin saint,
  That haunt the martyr's dream.

'And ah,' I said unto my white-robed guide,

'The rapture and the glory! might I speak

With one of those fair shapes, who float and glide

　　Like vapours round a peak.

' But who that glorious shade, of princely birth,

No less I deem him, who stalks forth alone ;

Some king he seems, who brooked not while on earth

　　A rival near his throne ? '

And she made earnest answer, ' That is he,

The Father and the Consul,* first and best

Of those who fought for Roman liberty,

　　And fighting sank to rest.

---

* Lucius Junius Brutus, one of the first two consuls.

' And now all men saw how Brutus loved his country, for he bade the lictors put all the traitors to death, and his own sons first, and men could mark in his face the struggle between his duty as chief magistrate of Rome, and his feelings as a father : and while they praised and admired him, they pitied him yet the more.'—Liddell's *History of Rome*, Book I.

' Happy, till on his heart the shadow fell

Of that his awful deed, so sternly great,

That he died crowned with woe unspeakable,

   A martyr for the state.

' Immortal patriot, well thy country's tears

Hailed thee reviver of her fire that slept,

When o'er thine urn those lights of ancient years,

   The Roman matrons wept !'

Loving I watched him as he past away,

And faded from me.—Next a chief drew near,*

With stern dark eyes that spoke of martial sway,

   And brow of noble cheer.

High-souled and calm, as when he sought his tomb

A self-made exile, and went forth alone,

Well-knowing that the hated city's doom

   Was purchased by his own.

  * Regulus. The story of his stern self-sacrifice is too well
known to need repetition here.

Feeling, perchance, a foretaste of the crown
Deathless for ever, when the might of Rome
Grown mightier, hurled her stately rival down,
    Queen of the wild sea-foam.

Thus hoping, he departed, glad to die,
So cold, among a people's prayers and tears,
Even his forsaken consort's passionate cry
    Rang faintly on his ears.

Him next I saw, in conscious strength sublime,
The Carthaginian leader ; such his fame,
Even the stern Roman in the olden time
    Had shuddered at his name.

And I stood breathless, while the voice rang out,
That cheered his Carthaginians many a day,
When following up the Roman battle-rout,
    Or linked in war-array.

'Those were great days of old, by Trebia's wave,*

And Thrasimene's shore,† when shield on shield

Clashed loud through blinding fog-wreaths, and the

    brave

      Fought horribly concealed.

'Or later, when the vanquished eagles fled,

Where Aufidus ran flushed with bloody rain,

And many a Roman mother wept her dead,

      Laid low on Cannæ's plain.

'Well might the voice of mourning shake the land,

The death-doomed veteran, battling ere he die,

Grasps not his blade more grimly in his hand

      Than I grasped Italy !

---

* The battle of the Trebia, fought 218 B.C., ended Hannibal's
first campaign.

† The battle of Lake Thrasimene, 217 B.C., was, as is well
known, fought in a thick mist. 'So hot was the conflict, that
the combatants did not feel the shock of an earthquake, which
overthrew many cities of Italy.'

'Alas, my brother, fallen in front of war,*

Thy country's anguish for thy funeral-pall,

Who mourned thee like a weeping queen, whose star

    Had only risen to fall.

'Yet deem not that I trembled on that day,

But self-possessed, and spurning dark Despair,

For four long years I sternly stood at bay,

    A lion in his lair.

'And when at last my sad old age of grief

Came on me, mourning Carthage and her woes,

My friendly signet brought me sweet relief,†

    And soothed me to repose.'

---

* The battle of the Metaurus, 207 B.C., where Hasdrubal fell fighting, delivered Rome from the power of her great rival, and was the death-blow to Hannibal's fortune.

        'Occidit, occidit

  Spes omnis et fortuna nostri

    Nominis, Hasdrubale interempto.'—*Horace*, Carm. IV. iv. 70.

† The great Carthaginian, to avoid falling into the hands of his implacable foes, swallowed a dose of poison, which, according

He ceased, but ere my reverent lips could frame
Fit answer, vanished ghost-like.   Next I saw
The foremost hero of those days of fame,
   When Athens' will was law.*

The god-like man, who loved through life's long
   years,
Though Christless, heavenly justice, somewhat stern,
And yet so noble, that his country's tears
   Fell hotly on his urn.

Feeling as one who mourns in deep distress
Neglected while in life, the fallen brave,
While sad rains for her past unfaithfulness
   Drop fruitless o'er his grave.

to the common story, he carried with him constantly in the
hollow of a ring.—Liddell's *Rome*, Book V.
  * Aristides the Just.

Him too, the flower of statesmen in his time,*
Who felt the galling shafts of dark disgrace
Pierce his proud soul, but conquering died sublime,
   And foremost in the race.

Bowed o'er his grave the Athenian matrons wept,
Whom death's drear Angel carried swift away
When most they loved him, mourning him who
    slept,
   Their glory and their stay.

Then came an old man,† with an eager throng,
Whereof each happy listener, like a child,
Drank in his utterance as he paced along,
   And as he spoke, he smiled.

So to the world unknown he past from Time,
Calm-musing on the threshold of the grave,
As when he roamed with Plato the sublime,
   By sweet Ilissus' wave.

      * Pericles.   † Socrates.

Then Phocion the ill-starred, whose fate was cast

In troubled waters, happier, had he known

To rise on high, not bow before the blast

   That swept him yielding down.

Loving I gazed on him, with love and awe

On his majestic rival,* whose sweet speech

Had power the hearts of men to melt and draw,

   And knit them each to each.

Rock-like that statesman, in the days of fear,

Rose o'er a sea of faces white with dread,

While from his lips fell silver-toned and clear

   Sounds that might rouse the dead.

As high above the surging crowd he stood,

While flashing through his eyes the soul-fire shone,

Denouncing with winged words that stir the blood,

   The Man of Macedon.

      * Demosthenes.

But ah ! the anguish of those sharp death-pains,

When on his track the fierce destroyer came ;

And the swift poison ran along the veins,

    And quenched that heart of flame.

Next with a sweet faint smile spoke unto me

A queen-like lady,* tall and fair of face,

I knew her by her calm proud majesty

    A dame of Roman race.

' Welcome, O happy stranger, angel-led,

Thrice blest, while breathing mortal breath, to go

Thro' temple-halls and chambers of the dead,

    Made happy after woe.

' Say, does the lofty memory still burn bright

In hearts of men, or has their love grown cold

For my two sons ? who fought the people's fight

    In those dark days of old,

        * Cornelia, the mother of the Gracchi.

' When Rome's o'ershadowing glory waned at last,

Down-tottering toward corruption, when she grew

Slothful and base, and mindless of the past,

   Ruled by the selfish few.

' My sons, my jewels, still my heart's true star,

In life so loving-faithful, burns the same,

As when of old I trained them for the war,

   And nursed them for their fame.'

' Alas, my sovereign lady,' I replied,

' Be the sad cypress, not the laurel-crown

Of this vain world their guerdon, for they died

   Not for their own renown.

' But they rose up to rend a people's chains,

And, careless of the servile crowd's applause,

Pressed toward the goal, and dared the martyr's

    pains,

   True to a noble cause.

' Yet, if thou yearn for praise of mortal breath,

Know that whene'er their names are named, again

Their high heroic virtue, conquering death,

   Thrills through the souls of men.'

' I marvel not,' she answered, while her eyes

Flashed out clear lightnings of immortal birth;

' Than their pure deaths no prouder destinies

   Await the sons of earth.'

Then, with a sweet smile of farewell, she left

My side, and through the fragrant vapours gray,

Like a fair swan through morning-clouds, she cleft

   Her silent onward way.

Him next I saw, the god-like Florentine,

The glory of his race, his features wrought

Into a calm austere, and half divine,

   By strength of earnest thought.

Her too, the warrior maiden, who uprose
The champion of down-trodden France, and fell
By grace of God, the foremost among those
    Who love their country well.

Savonarola, his fine brain on fire
With visionary musings, yet withal
So loving, that upon his martyr pyre
    He heard the angels' call.

And mild Corregio, his warm brain still rife
With heavenly shapes whose glory makes us start,
Virgin, and Saint, and Child, that thronged in life
    His beauty-haunted heart.

But my sad thoughts flew back to earlier days,
I saw him stoop beneath his shameful load,*
Toiling towards doom beneath the pitiless rays
    That pierced him while they glowed.

---

    * He is said to have been paid in copper for his last picture, the Assumption of the Virgin, in the cupola of the Cathedral at Parma, and to have died soon after carrying the unworthy load home to his family under the burning Italian sun. The truth of this story, however, has been questioned.

Yet he forgot the wrath of burning skies,

And all his cruel wrongs, and bitter loss,

Remembering how, through greater agonies,

   One greater bore his cross.

Great-hearted Luther, who stood forth alone

His church's destined champion from his youth,

From whose stern lips burst like a trumpet-tone

   The gospel words of Truth.

Tasso, the suffering poet, his sweet strains

Thrilled through the heart o' the world, but could not

    save

Their minstrel, drawn by galling prison-chains

   Down to a glorious grave.

There too, deep-musing on the days of old,

And deeds of high emprise on unknown seas,

Strode on, with haughty tread, and bearing bold,

   The glorious Genoese.*

             * Columbus.

His was the sad proud destiny to wear

The cypress-laurel wreath that glory flings

O'er her most cherished children, and to bear

   The perilous scorn of kings.

And wilt thou sail no more to sapphire skies,

Nor cheer with glorious speech thy murmuring

    band ?

Wilt watch no more with ever-yearning eyes

   For that long-wished-for land ?

Yet the glad tides that lave the golden street

Shall soothe thy woe-worn spirit evermore,

With sounds more blessed than even the waves that

    beat

   On yonder Western shore.

Then those two brother martyrs of great name,*

True followers in the path that Stephen trod,

---

* Ridley and Latimer. 'We shall this day, my lord,' said
Latimer to Ridley at the stake, 'light such a candle in England
as shall never be extinguished.'

Supremely blessed, for smiling 'mid the flame
   They gave themselves to God.

Then More, who knew this life was nothing worth,
Yet nobly worked its work, though glad to fling
The burden from his soul, and quit the earth,
   His conscience for his king.

Raleigh, whose dazzling sun of glory rose
To set in gloom, not stainless, for his soul
Nursed fiery thoughts, that left him no repose,
   But spurred him towards the goal.

All these great souls, whose memories, glory-fraught,
Because they quailed not in life's solemn wars,
Stir the heart's blood, pressed onward, wrapt in
    thought,
   And silent as the stars.

And ah,' I thought, 'how glorious 'twere to die,
So might I move these happy shades among,
And from their own lips hear each history
   Of conflict 'gainst the wrong.'

Even as I spoke, I saw a stately shade,
Who silent from his fellows stalked apart ;
A heavenly grace upon his features played,
   That shone into my heart.

As on some fair Greek god, who evermore
Broods speechless in the marble, even so,
Supremely calm, the glory that he wore
   Slept on his brow of snow.

Soul-struck I hurried towards him, and I said,
' O thou, so awful in thy majesty,
Tell me thy name, thou king among the dead,'
   He answered, ' I am he—

'Falkland, unhappy, for my life was thrown

Into a raging sea, by war-bolts riven,

A yawning gulf of woe, that dragged me down

   From thoughts that towered to heaven.

'My course I steered through shades of blackest night,

Without one hope of refuge or release,

Till in the welcome tumult of the fight

   The death-shot brought me peace.

'Yet deem not that I murmur at my fate,

Nor that my early doom, so sad and stern;

Who would not smile at death to serve the state,

   Has still God's truth to learn!'

I listened, but the pulses of my life

Thrilled, for I hung impassioned on his words,

And yearned to hurl myself into the strife,

   And die among the swords.

Then Galileo, who with sunward flight
Upsoaring, Nature's volume dared unroll,
And, fallen on days of darkness, hailed the light
   That flooded all his soul.

So he lived calm near Arno's snowy walls,
As one who on some mountain's crown at rest,
Hears far beneath the plunging waterfalls
   Chafe like a sea distrest.

And he grew glad to wear his crown of woe,
And spurned the vulgar crowd's ignoble hate,
Feeling the God within him, and the glow
   Known only to the great.

With him the Master of the heaven-toned lyre,
The mild majestic Milton, paced along ;
They held communion sweet in words of fire,
   Converse of stars and song.

Those two had met ere now, when Death on one,

Old Age's friend, was stealing on a-pace,*

The other setting forward, like the sun,

   Girt for his glorious race.

Nor knowing that he too was doomed at last,

Like him he gazed on, with ethereal blade

To cleave his way through foemen round him massed,

   Serene and undismayed.

Then came another, whose unstained renown

Shines pure as snow on mountains, for he saw

With falcon-glance the future of the Crown,

   That dared defy the Law.

Honour to Hampden's earnest soul, who first

Made the great heart of mighty England glow

With that fierce wrath, foredoomed on those to burst

   Who sought to lay her low.

  * Milton and Galileo met in Italy in 1638. 'There it was,
that I found and visited the famous Galileo, grown old, a pri-
soner to the Inquisition.'

Another chieftain, whose bright fame shall last
Eternal as the memory of his woes,
Came slowly stalking on, but ere he past
   King-like, I knew Montrose.

Then Russell—like the thunderbolt from gloom,
His death-scene flashed upon me.   Clear and loud,
The stern accuser's voice, denouncing doom,
   Rang o'er the surging crowd.

But he stood statue-like, with calm proud eyes,
Lit with the glorious truths for which he died,
While she,* the consort of his agonies,
   Sat death-white by his side.

Unto death faithful, though at times the tears
Stain her cheek's snowy marble, when the Past
Rises, with all its happy hateful years,
   Those years, too sweet to last.

     * That sweet saint who sat by Russell's side
       Under the judgment-seat.—ROGERS, *Human Life.*

O the wild joy, the throbbing fever-heat
Of youth's first passion mantling on the brow!
Alas, poor wanderer with the clay-cold feet,
   Where is thy true love now?

But a sweet voice upon my spirit fell
In low soft accents, tremulous and deep,
'Mourn not, for I and my beloved dwell
   Where Christ hath given us sleep.'

Then from the thickening shadows lifted up,
One solemn shape rose slowly on my sight,*
With thin wan hands that held a poison-cup,
   Then vanished into night.

I knew the princely soul, the wondrous boy,
The young Apollo, whose melodious rhyme
Had echoed through the world in waves of joy,
   Resounding through all time.

       * Chatterton.

But Famine, at the dawn of life's fair day,

Touched him with icy fingers, till the strain,

That might have thrilled creation, died away

    In one long wail of pain.

Over a stormy sea his bark was driven,

Yet well I trust his spirit had found grace,

When, after death, the pitying light of heaven

    Fell on his pale proud face.

Then came a queen, with stately steps and slow ;

More than thy careless, laughter-loving glance,

I love those sweet gold tresses white with woe,

    O martyred Bride of France !

    .   .   .   .   .   .

Now my heart throbbed with joys of heavenly birth,

And passionate thoughts, and deep imaginings,

' Ah, might I burst the narrowing bonds of earth,

    And mount on eagle wings !

' Then my strong spirit, with a towering flight,

Should spurn life's barriers. Not a thousand wars

Can quell the heroic soul, that yearns for light,

   And struggles toward the stars.'

But the fair Angels answered, ' Thou hast known

The bliss of souls victorious over pains ;

Wait therefore, and toward God's eternal throne

   Press on, while life remains.

' So Life's strange harp, with its wild chords of

       gladness,

So loved and cherished by the careless throng,

Shall yield a music of celestial sadness,

   Surpassing human song.

' And those whom blissful Death has heavenward

       drawn,

Rejoicing in heroic agonies,

Feel their white faces flushing with the dawn

   That breaks on Paradise.'

Then 'mid a waving, as of spirit-hands,

　The Temple and the Angels past away ;

I stood alone, where on broad meadow-lands

　Blazed down the shafts of day.

MARATHON.

My Athens, thou hast fallen,

Yet, lonely as thou art,

The memory of the days of old,

Shall cheer thy mourning heart.

The glory of the dead who fell

In the ancient giant time,

When bards' thoughts flashed like the bolts of heaven

From thunder-clouds of rhyme,

And flung such a dazzling crown of light

On our heroes as they lay,

That they slept, as yon red sun sleeps in his might,

In his loved Piræus bay.

As Zeus among the immortal Gods,

More mighty and more blest,

As the glad morning-star's fresh power

Shines brighter than the rest,

So far above the fields of fame

In ancient years that shone,

Shines the day when the Persians fled to their ships,

From the field of Marathon.

The haughty Persian monarch

Had sent his heralds forth,

' Search me the stubborn land of Greece,

Search her from south to north.

The mainland and the islands

Washed by the Ægean wave,

That sea accurst, whence the black storm burst,

Where my proud fleet found a grave.

Tell Sparta and tell Athens,

Tell every warrior Greek,

Darius, the great Persian,

By us hath deigned to speak.

Bow down to him at our commands,

And earth and water bring;

'Twere wiser to face the wrath of heaven,

Than the wrath of Persia's king!'

Forth sailed the chosen heralds,

Borne by the glad wind's breath:

Little they deemed that the favouring gales

Were wafting them to death.

Short answer made our countrymen,

Our stalwart sires of old,

But it froze the heralds' blood in their veins,

And their lips grew icy cold.

Straight from the council chamber

They went down to the grave;

So perished they in the olden time

Who called the Greek a slave.

In silken Susa's palace

The great King lay at ease,

But Fame's swift breath bore the message of death
Far o'er the deep blue seas.
He and his twenty satraps
By all the Gods have sworn,
' On the hated Greek full soon to wreak
The whirlwind of our scorn.

' Pallas shall shudder in her shrine,
And the Greek maidens moan,
And Sparta's sons shall tremble,
And Athens' warriors groan,
When the wrath of the fiery Persian
Shall thunder o'er the main ;
Woe to the bloody nation,
Woe for the heralds slain !'

High swelled the shout of triumph,
Loud the barbarian boast,
When the flower of Persia's chivalry
Set sail from Persia's coast.

All sworn to carry fire and sword

O'er the smiling Attic plains,

To burn our homes to ashes,

And bind our sons in chains.

As swans in flight majestic

Float with the freshening gale,

So steered round Parnes' rugged steep

The Persian fleet full sail.

The Attic shepherd saw the ships

From the lonely mountain height,

And forthwith long red tongues of fire

Shot forth into the night;

And all that night in Athens,

Were hurrying to and fro,

For they knew those harbingers of flame,

And armed them for the foe.

At break of day, the People

Have met in stern debate,

Short space had they for counsel,

For War was at the gate.

But though dark death and slavery

Thus stared them in the face,

Not a man for the wealth of Lydia's lord

That morn had changed his place.

For they felt quick-pulsing through their veins

The old heroic blood,

Had a wretch shown a sign of dastard fear,

They had stoned him where he stood.

And they have marshalled forth their host,

And chosen Generals ten,

All skilled to sway on the battle-day

The rush of armèd men.

And all, save babes and women,

And grey old men, are gone;

By noon the Athenian army

Had marched for Marathon.

G

Long watched they the bright armour
Far flashing through the dust,
Then turned them to the blessed Gods
On whom they built their trust;
To Zeus, the great Olympian,
They breathed an earnest prayer,
And they called on virgin Pallas
To shield them from despair.

Meanwhile the great Ten Thousand
Moved on with banners spread,
And helmets glittering in the sun,
And firm and measured tread.
They struggled up the mountains
That on the plain look down,
And saw the white tents of the Persian,
And thought on their old renown.

Callimachus the Archon
Was chieftain of the Ten,
And he hath called his colleagues,
Those great and earnest men:

Long time they sat in council,

Till the stars rose o'er the height,

And the tents on the plain, and the ships on
   the main,

Lay shrouded by the night.

Then spoke the good Miltiades

His counsel sage and bold,

' Dread not the Persian weapons,

But dread the Persian gold.

Ill fares the camp or city

Where gold can make its way ;

Ever on eve of battle

The traitor loves delay.

Upon them, ere our good swords rust.

And treason works us woe ;

Drive the barbarian to the sea

Ere the next sunset glow ! '

Each of the great Ten Generals

Took order for a day,

And last the brave Miltiades

Hath marshalled his array.

I ween the Athenians' heart beat high,

When they saw the Persian host,

Like huge waves topped with glittering spray,

Move slowly from the coast.

There rushed the jewelled Persian,

Spurring his battle steed,

And there the warrior Sacian

And there the haughty Mede.

Far, far to west the Carians,

All burning for the fight,

And there the Lydian myriads

Shone like a sea of light.

But like a swooping eagle,

That from the hill-top springs,

Came down the Athenian army

With rush of mighty wings.

Right desperate was the onset
When, rushing face to face,
The Greek and the barbarian
Closed in a stern embrace.

Shrill clashed the clanging falchions,
And fell the bloody rain,
And Death, the ghastly reaper,
Bore harvest of the slain.
Then rose the ringing war-shout,
As when wild waves wake from sleep,
And when lurid Night with her red storm-light
Comes thundering from the deep.

Then, as a wave reluctant
Sweeps seaward with a roar,
Fell back the Athenian centre
Retreating from the shore.
But on the right Miltiades,
The chieftain of the fray,

And on the left Callimachus,

Have held our foes at bay.

Before the sharp Greek broad-sword

The soft barbarians yield,

The right wing and the left wing

Have chased them from the field.

Then our great Captain's voice rang out

O'er the tumult of the war,

' See ye yon Persian lancers

Come spurring from afar ?

Well have ye fought, my brothers,

Throughout this bloody day,

Well pleased might Zeus and Ares

Look down on such a fray.

' Leave we yon routed foemen,

Yon rude and broken mass,

Leave them to struggle in the marsh,

And treacherous morass.

There let them idly perish,

The slaves of guilt and fear,

But strike ye one more stroke for me

And all your hearts hold dear,

For swift as death the Persian

Comes rushing on our rear!'

As down Thessalian mountains

Thunders the falling snow,

So fell the fierce Athenians

Upon the faltering foe.

Flashed like a gleam of lightning,

The Greek sword from the sheath,

Fell on the Persian's turban,

And clove him to the teeth.

With faces deadly white thro' fear,

And curses on their lips,

As wolves before Molossian hounds,

They chased them to the ships.

The battle raged till sunset,

But when the day grew dark,

The star-beams glanced on cloven helms,

And corpses stiff and stark.

As when Zeus hangs his rainbow

Athwart the stormy sky,

So lay by the side of the roaring tide

The Persian chivalry.

A voice of lamentation

In Susa's royal street,

' Where be our splendid satraps,

And where our gallant fleet ?

Chant, chant the Carian death-dirge,

O lonely Lydian maids !

For the haughty souls of our heroes

Have gone down to the shades.'

But joy to thee, fair Athens !

For the great deeds thou hast wrought,

Ne'er, since our warring world began,
Hath such a fight been fought.

Glory to those who the grave's dark path
For their country's weal have trod,
Glory to thee, Miltiades,
Thou tutelary god !
And for the brave that slumber
Upon the sacred plain,
The might of breathing marble
Shall make them live again :
The painting, and the trophy,
The Poet's loftiest tone,
Shall tell to future ages
The day of Marathon ;
To endless generations
In thunder-peals shall speak,
Death to the coward Persian,
And glory to the Greek!

DANTE.

FROM far Italian skies the shadows steal
O'er Arno's banks, whereon the soft waves sob ;
At eve I gaze upon those banks and feel
 Their Poet's pulsing throb.

Ah, still beneath the tossing tide of time,
Heaves the swift under-current of bright thought,
Still glows the vestal fire of bards sublime,
 By whom great songs were wrought.

And still the heavenly Poet, free from woe,
High o'er the shock of warring tempests stands,
Watching the crowd of strugglers far below,
 From Christ's own table-lands.

More than the rest he suffers in his time,
As He best knoweth who hath made him strong,
And given him grace to hurl the shafts of rhyme,
   And war against the wrong.

Round convent-walls, where moss and ivy cling,
Dome, tower, and stately palace grouped beneath
In charmed repose, the happy mountains fling
   Their olive-garden wreath.

And holy San Miniato towers in air,
From whose long aisles, by reverent votaries trod,
The soft Italian night-wind wafts the prayer
   Unto the gate of God.

The Apennines lie smiling on my sight,
And moonlit Florence sleeps beneath my feet.
Towards yon far cloud my spirit wings her flight,
   Where sky and mountains meet.

Where dwell the great Twin souls,—the glorious
    pair—
The Poet and his bride,—the happy dead ?—
Float their free spirits through calm fields of air,
    Of old they loved to tread ?

Or in some heavenly valley, where the wind
Blows soft from shadowy summits, warmly kissed
By a mellow dying glory, lie reclined,
    Veiled in a purple mist ?

Six hundred solemn years have fled since first,
Shrined in a boyish shape, a soul grew strong,
A mighty heart, from whence in fulness burst
    The majesty of song.

From moaning waves he drew the voice of grief,
Power from the cloud where sleeping thunder lies,
And melancholy from the cypress-leaf,
    And rapture from blue skies.

And as a suffering saint, whose sacred tears
Foretell the coming glow of heavenly grace,
He bore his glorious fate in future years
    Foreshadowed on his face.

For he was one of those, who from their birth
Wearing the crown of immortality,
Have sorrow for their portion here on earth,
    And glory when they die.

So felt he his great soul within him grow
From strength to strength, in majesty and might,
Attuned alike to tenderest tones of woe,
    And passionate delight.

For a fair girl he felt the deep love start,
As when a limned Madonna charms a saint,
A spiritual impulse of the heart,
    Pure from all earthly taint.

I see an old man lifted up on high,*
I see the white-robed myriads throng the street;
Rung every dome, and pillared sanctuary,
　　With clang of echoing feet.

And great church-organs thrilled the ponderous arch,
And silver trumpets blared a loud acclaim,
And mail-clad warriors joined the measured march,
　　With solemn looks of shame.

But one lone Poet spirit stood apart,
On his grim features played a wondrous scorn,
Strong words of truth burst from his great good heart
　　Fresh as the wind at morn.

And, as the stern Bard sang, the Infernal Gate
Shook, and the full air throbbed with angels' wings.
For falsehood quailed before the voice of Fate,
　　When Dante swept the strings !

---

* Dante was present at the Jubilee held at Rome by Pope
Boniface, A.D. 1300, and inveighed against the errors of the
Papal religion during his stay.

Arm for the war, thou gallant Florentine ;

Hurl the light lance, and spur the flying steed ;

Yet deem not that proud Fame thy wreath shall twine,

    From fields where warriors bleed.

Thine be the laurelled crown of ancient years,

Old Homer's massive brow divinely wore ;

Thine the bright thoughts that, pure as angels' tears,

    Fall from the heavenly shore.

Yet shalt thou wander forth a man exiled

From thine own hearth, and Arno's lonely strand

Shall hear the vexed waves murmuring for their child,

    An outcast from the land.

Perish the soul that sows the seeds of hate !

Whence the rank weeds of civil discord spring,

And those brave hearts that should have served the

        State,

    Fight for an upstart king.

Perish the day when Florence grasped the sword,
Rose like a wave, and bore away the right,
Like a proud steed, that bears his shuddering lord
   Unto an endless night.

An everlasting blot is on thy name,
Florence, ungrateful mother of the great!
For our dark story drop the tears of shame,
   Thy banished Poet's fate.

Where Santa Croce's convent sleeps apart,
With stern grey walls that frown o'er desolate plains,
Hallowed for ever,—there an exile's heart
   Found solace in his strains.

There to the glorious phantoms of the brain
From the realities of life he fled,
And, wandering through the realms of guilt and pain,
   Held converse with the dead;

Or borne on wings of light he soared afar,

And, musing on the Majesty intense,

Broke through the clouds, and pierced the mists
that bar

Our duller mortal sense.

In visionary grief he lost his own,

And holy peace was his, and sweet content,

Yet oft for Florence came the tear and groan,

And musical lament.

' My heart,' he sang, ' is like a dreary wave

That washes on a wild and lonely shore ;

And darkness, like the darkness of the grave,

Broods o'er me evermore.

An aching void, a dull cold weight of pain,

A burning thirst for victory never won,

A chilling sense of toil endured in vain,

Of earnest work undone,—

All these have power upon me—till my heart
Thrilled through with anguish, yearns to flee away,
And pants for rest, forbidden to depart,
  Fettered by bonds of clay.

And ever o'er this tumult of my breast
Float thoughts of those I love where'er I roam,
As lights and shadows from the reddening East
  Glance o'er the rough sea-foam.

And Florence rises like a pictured saint
Crown'd with pale moonlight, or the glimmering
    ghost
Of a dead bride, that with low words and faint
  Speaks of a land loved most.

O Florence, well-beloved in days of old!
Now longed for, as I long to rest with God,
Though thy fair streets, to me grown strange and
    cold,
  By alien feet are trod.

O men of iron heart and ruthless hand,
Ye drained my life-blood when ye thrust me forth,
And ye have made me like a desert land,
    Cold as the frozen North !

Ye hear the Poet's thoughts of thunder sound,
Know that such dread songs pierce the parent mind,
Fierce shafts of Fate, rejoicing to rebound,
    And strike their sovereign blind.

And though the high Bard scale the Eternal gate,
Far o'er the struggling crowd on strong wings borne,
Swift from the crashing thunder-clouds of hate
    Flash forth the fires of scorn.

Yet I trust on—though tears of blood they weep,
Tossed on life's tempest-heaving tide of woes,
Clasped in Death's loving arms, the great shall sleep,
    In most sublime repose.

What though no earthly laurel crown the bust
Of earnest souls, that toil beneath the sun,
Nor let the sharp steel of their genius rust,
   Till Christ's good fight be won.

High thoughts and noble deeds, that breathe around
The Poet's heavenward steps, shall guard the dead,
And make their fame a consecrated ground,
   Where no base feet dare tread.

And pure old age the golden fruit shall reap,
Which God hath willed for those that travel far,
More blest than babes, whom angels kiss to sleep,
   Unsoiled by dust of war.

Whate'er men say, the Poet cannot die ;
For though his dull material life depart,
His living spiritual mastery
   Thrills through the great world's heart.

Our children's children round my grave shall tell

How Dante fought for faith and truth divine;

' Here lies the Bard who sang of Heaven and Hell :

   God rest the Florentine !'

Where finds the wanderer o'er life's dreary wave,

A sheltering haven, and a last repose,

Where the blest spot, made grander by his grave,

   And holier by his woes?

Where o'er the sea a city's bulwarks smile,

Ravenna's white walls washed by Adria's tide,

A blameless Poet, pure and free from guile,

   As he had lived, he died.

As some strong war-ship breasts the waves all day,

But furls her shattered sails when near the shore,

Majestically calm he past away

   From where he wept before.

Close the pure eyes, and bring the robe of snow,

Lay out the clay-cold corpse upon the bier,

Gaze for the last time on the massive brow,—

   More than a king lies here.

But we must part—the Day-God puts to flight

The shades that grouped where the glad moonbeams

    fell,

And Florence wakes.—To Dante and the night

   I breathe a proud farewell.

MODERN ITALY.*

Though now from Jove's Olympian peak
   No more the bolts are hurled,
Nor thine imperial senate speak
   In thunder through the world,
All human hearts to thee are fled,
Thou mother of the mighty dead!

Not that the light of ancient crowns
   Gilds thy declining day,
Nor that thy Coliseum frowns
   In passionate decay,
And shows the majesty of fate,
The glory of the fallen great.

* This poem was written some years ago, during the occupation of Rome by the French. Recent events have verified Mrs. Browning's prediction, 'The future of Italy shall not be disinherited.'

But that Italia builds her trust
  On deathless days of old,
And sacred Freedom fires her dust
  That lay for ages cold,
Through war-smoke, and through senate's strife,
From those sharp throes she starts to life.

The great world views thy second birth,
  As Light of later times,
Thou ancient empress of the earth,
  And Ruler of the climes!
Thy soul hath felt the chains too long,
Immortal nurse of art and song!

Thy great allies are God above,
  The sympathy of states,
And England's ever-faithful love,
  That conquers or creates.
Deep based on sand, not on the rock,
What despot force shall face the shock!

Long o'er thy buried grandeur's site,
   Thy sepulchre of kings,
Two grim and ghastly birds of night
   Have flapped their sable wings,
Two vultures, born in evil hour,
The Austrian sway, the papal power.

But they have mourned their shattered yoke,
   Their veil of night withdrawn,
When from the rolling war-clouds broke
   The death-fires of the dawn,
That glowed on Solferino's heath,
And dark Magenta's field of death.

Then came there One, whose soaring flight
   No tyrant's frown could quell,
Whose rush was like a whirlwind's might,
   And shook the gates of hell ;
A blameless knight and free from guile,
That hero of the lonely isle.

Let Naples chant triumphal strains
    For liberty restored,
And rescued captives break the chains
    That bound them to their lord,—
The generous Prince, who freely gave
To all a dungeon and a grave.

Go, base son of a baser sire!
    But learn, ere thou depart,
How great a hatred can inspire
    An injured people's heart,
And deem not that Caëta's gate
Shall bar thy swift avenging Fate.

The clouds must thunder o'er the deep
    Before the sky be calm,
And Italy the thorns must reap,
    Ere she can grasp the palm,—
Must feel, ere she the brand can sheathe,
More than the bitterness of death.

For we have seen her doomed to play
 The Spartan mother's part,
To wrest the chieftain's sword away
 She welcomed to her heart,
And see him wounded and alone
In Spezzia's sullen walls of stone.

The shades of utter darkness grow
 Around Saint Peter's chair,
The empty pomp, the solemn show,
 Are melting into air.
The ring, the crozier, and the keys,—
Hath the world stooped to things like these?

And thou, stern chieftain of the Gauls,
 So silent and discreet!
Why float thy banners on Rome's walls,
 Thy soldiers throng her street?
To Brennus' fame dost thou aspire?
' Woe to the vanquished ' thy desire?

We know that monarchs can betray,
 And statesmen can deceive;
But, God defend the right! we pray,
 Nor tremble as we leave
Our hopes—our fears—our love with thee,
Regenerated Italy!

109

A POLISH LAMENT.

O for the days when we were strong!
  Before our fathers fell asleep,
When Freedom fired the sons of song;
  'Tis long since we have learned to weep.
Aye, weep those bitter maddening tears,
Whose memory fades not with the years.

My spirit soars to those proud days
  When Poles might die, but never yield;
The well-stormed city's funeral blaze,
  The shivered spear, the shattered shield.
The glory from those bright years thrown,
Is all we *now* may call our own.

But we shall see Sarmatia rise,

 Lift from her burning martyr-pile

Her pale proud face, and hail the skies

 Exultant with a heavenly smile.

For well I trust we were not born

The slaves of everlasting scorn.

And tell me not that Freedom dies ;

 The tales of fights fought long ago

Still call the lightnings from our eyes,

 Dash o'er our cheeks a crimson glow ;

Still flash through our sad hearts the fires

Breathed from our warrior-poets' lyres.

Sarmatia's brow was crowned with palm,

 What time Zamoyski led our van ; *

* 'For his success in this astonishing campaign, in which he
had annihilated rather than routed a great army of Tartars,
Zamoyski was enthusiastically cheered by the diet of the
republic.'—*History of Poland.*

All Europe shook, but we were calm,
  And rushing on the Tartar Khan,
We hurled his routed myriads back,
With death and ruin on their track.

Three hearts,* in Cracow's Minster fair,
  Lie hushed—how proudly sleep the brave,
Where solemn psalm and patriot prayer
  Rise constantly! though o'er their grave
The mists of many years are shed,
Green are the laurels of our dead.

At sunset, for a little space,
  Our Leader on the Turks gazed down,
And a strange light lit up the face
  Of that great chief of high renown.
He felt the wave of victory
Surge through his soul's majestic sea.

* Sobieski, Kosciusko, Poniatowski.

Through centuries of shame and loss,
   Our Sobieski's star shines clear;
High o'er the crescent flamed the cross,
   When flashed his dread avenging spear.
Let hardly saved Vienna sing
The glory of our hero-king!

But O fair Warsaw, cypress-crowned,
   Where our last chief the last time bled,
Art thou not ever-sacred ground
   Blest field, where fought our glorious dead?
In vain, in vain, Sarmatia fell!
How live they, those who love her well?

Scarce second he, the Prince who drew
   A patriot's sword that day, then past
To where Gaul's baffled eagles flew
   From Moscow-fires, and found at last—
What nobler boon for noble pride?—
A grave by Kosciusko's side.

Well know I, when the death-fire glares,

    When our true sons their war-steeds urge,

And through our foemen's broken squares

    Our white-plumed storm of horsemen surge,

They will be with us on that day,

As erst on banks of Vistula!

Hark! the dread voices call to fight,

    We must avenge, not mourn, our woes;

Let us rush onward for our right,

    As down the rent crag roar the snows!

No more, my brothers, let us weep,

But Christ for Poland, and strike deep!

ASPIRATIONS.

Let us not stagnate, let our quickened blood
Rove through its channels like a troubled sea
Lashed by strong whirlwinds.   Till the golden flood
  Of calm eternity

Absorbs all changes, let us never change,
And let the immortal through the mortal shine;
Let us from what is human onward range
  To that which is divine.

For when I look upon this age's spoils,
The pride of arms, the march of intellect,
I care not, by these everlasting toils
  If life itself be checked.

That so the spirit may mount high above

The upward straining of our mortal clay,

All earthly knowledge by celestial love

  Being purged and done away.

FAREWELL STANZAS.

THOUGHTS of the lost, the loved, the dear,
Like Eden flowers around us cling.
Ah, what were earth without a tear?
A barren sand without a spring.

For those sweet rains that fall so fast
From heavy-clouded hearts and sad,
May leave us, for a pain that's past,
A grief that almost makes us glad.

We miss her, when the wintry sun
Flings o'er the foam his blood-red robe,
When all too slow the harsh hours run,
And slumber shrouds the silent globe.

We miss her, when through summer leaves

The stars peep, and the wild waves' song

On lone shores musically grieves,

And melancholy gusts wail long.

Yet peace floats o'er me when I feel

Communion of the earth and sea,

And o'er my mourning spirit steal

Sweet sounds that breathe of Heaven—and thee.

Though storm-tost seas may rage between,

One constant star shall never set,

But light thee with a love unseen,

And charm thee with a fond regret.

Oft shall I seem to lay my head

On thy sweet bosom, as of old,

And the dear voice of years long dead

Ring through my memory, clear and cold.

Then shall the tears of true love start,—
Of love, that may not change nor cloy,
And that deep sorrow of my heart
Be mellowed into mournful joy.

Ah, happy tears that gently flow,
Ah, holy fount of joy divine,
And deem not 'tis an idle woe
That links this last lament of mine.

For grand truths in such partings dwell,
Sprung from a pure, a heavenly birth,
They warn us eloquently well,
' Love was not made alone for earth.'

THOUGHTS ON LIFE.

In mine own heart I felt this truth,
Let others rave in idle verse,
That pleasures perish, and a curse
Lurks in the throbbing veins of youth.

Muse we where Titian's virgin gold
Shines upon Mary's holy head,
Draw precepts from the painted dead,
And sermons from the saints of old.

Then, like the rough waves stilled by Christ,
Our fever'd brain shall feel a calm,
And purged by spiritual balm
Our soaring eyes shall pierce the mist.

So sweet surmise shall vanquish Hate,
And, trust me, there shall come an hour,
When ripe with rolling years, the power
Of God's dear love shall conquer Fate.

Move on, thou sacred sun and moon,
Sublimely patient, still the same,
Enlighten with thy silent flame
The doubting hearts that faint too soon.

Thy tongues of fire shall teach the proud,
'Not soon can perfect knowledge grow,
Like that most perishable glow
That faints and dies on yonder cloud.

' Like us, be constant ; still thy fears,
Till from the quickened earth shall fall
Time's mantle, and the funeral pall
Drop from the fair face of the years.

' Press onward, though with care and crimes
The great world quiver to the root,
And pluck the age's flying fruit,
And reap the harvest of the times.

' For Duty, though ere morning light
Severe as frozen snow she seems,
Shall storm the gate of golden dreams
About the fourth watch of the night.'

AN ITALIAN SERENADE.

CLOSED lie the lustrous eyes, Heaven's deep blue
    scorning,
And as Day's sweet star, lighting on the billow,
Breaks through the cloudy twilight of the morning,
The bright head rests upon the snowy pillow.

For her the glowworm lights her lamp of amber,
When wandering far through tangled wildernesses;
The fairy fireflies flit about her chamber,
And wanton with her loose hair's golden tresses.

Yet wake, and hear thy Poet's mournful numbers,
While yet these summer nights are free from sor-
    row,
O may no voice of anguish break thy slumbers,
Nor calm day bring a passionate to-morrow!

Wake, while away thy Minstrel's steps are hasting,

And be one tender thought of him the token

Of future joy, and glory everlasting,

The Heaven of happy hearts, and faith unbroken.

' LA MADONE DE SAINT-SIXTE.'

Not all in vain the Italian spirit glows,
When gazing with a rapture of the heart,
On thy pure eyes, lit up with glorious woes,
Madonna mine, all holy as thou art.

Before that brow divine we may not kneel,
Nor bow the head in nobly humble prayer,
Yet our lone breasts the rays of light may feel,
That God himself hath consecrated there.

And that sweet sorrow on thy fair face shed,
May teach Christ's drooping babes to bear the
    cross,
To follow where thy gentle soul hath led,
So shall our loss be gain, our gain our loss.

O let thy beauty, passionless and pure,

Breathe o'er us like a long-forgotten strain,

That we may learn to suffer and endure,

May feel the immortal joy of heavenly pain.

AD ——.

As when a painter in the moonlight stands,
And muses on a grand ideal face,
His pencil trembling in his earnest hands,
And clasps the vision with a soul's embrace.

Yet weeps, for his weak spirit yearns in vain,
To shape and colour what he deems so fair,
My thoughts, dear ——, feel the self-same pain,
And pant for utterance with the same despair.

For though thy memory, like some heavenly tune,
Breathe thoughts of light that pierce our world's
     eclipse,
Like fresh flowers blasted by the breath of noon,
The faint words fade and die upon my lips.

And so my love becomes a silent dream,

Yet not less pure, eternal, or intense,

Than if the language of my heart could stream

In strains too high for earth, too sweet for sense.

ON AN ITALIAN PORTRAIT.

Lady of light ! thy loveliness on me
Shines fair and pure, as gleams the morning star
Over the dreary wastes of wintry sea,
On seamen from their own land wandering far.

The Poet, yearning through each golden year
To clothe impassioned thoughts in burning words,
Could wish no sweeter sorrow than to hear
Thy grand voice faint and die among the chords.

Let nobler singers, loftier minstrels, chant
Immortal praises for thy face divine,
In that voluptuous clime, where artists pant
To grace ideal nymphs with charms like thine.

Be it enough for me to stand apart,

To watch the soft glow of thy heavenly hair,

Or hear thy glorious laughter thrill my heart,

As silvery fountains cool the summer air.

SAPPHO.

FAITHFUL through twice a thousand years,
The Lesbian waves for Sappho long;
Such the sweet spell of tuneful tears,
And such the force of passion's song.
Through breathless calm or tempest-shock,
They woo the well-belovèd rock.

Sometimes they glow with lightning fires,
As she with frenzied love—sometimes
Their weary waywardness desires
The calm that sleeps in Sappho's rhymes.
They mirror in their restless roll,
The changes of that earnest soul.

'Ah woe;' they sing, 'the Great Tenth Muse,
Her face some envious spirit bars,
But surely she will not refuse
To gaze on us from yonder stars!
Drop down, O Queen divine, and dart
Deep, deep into our loving heart!

'Where Ocean smiles with southern gales,
Or golden sunlight's noonday swoon,
The rapture of his strange sea-tales
Shall charm thy faithless Phaon soon;
For we have strains of soothing might,
And everlasting as the light.'

But Sappho on her cloudy throne
Sits calm through twice a thousand years,
She may not move, but broods alone,
And drinks the music of the spheres.
Reads in the grand star-lettered page
The secrets of the golden age.

While ever round the rock's rough base

The wild waves moan eternally,

' Once more upon thy glowing face,

O Sappho, may we gaze and die ! '

All human hearts with Time wax cold,

But Ocean's love grows never old.

ANTIGONE.

THE brow a frozen snowdrift, and the face
Cold as the Phidian Pallas, the calm eyes,
Two heavenly harbingers of high resolve,
Lustrous and large as Hera's, not cast down,
Up-gazing with a passionate earnestness,
As if they searched the stars of heaven for light
In utter darkness; but anon a flush
Crimsons the white serenity of woe,
Sudden as lightning, for the deep love pants,
Like Phœbus' war steeds, when his chariot-wheels
Race o'er the rough ridge of the morning cloud,
Then all is calm, as when the sunset hues
Die from the face of an Italian heaven.

Ah, fair Greek girl ! thy patient gaze of pain

Haunts my charmed spirit, like a glimmering ghost

That may not rest, but wails eternally

Upon the golden threshold of the dawn.

SONG.

As those deceitful winds that blow
O'er poisoned blossoms, faint with death,
As streams that in the sunlight glow,
  Nor reck the worn stones strewn beneath.

So laughing Love, that veils the pain
Of passion, chills the thwarted heart,
Yet the deep music's maddening strain
That breathes within, will not depart.

And we live on as beats the wave
For ever lashed by blasting wind ;—
Live on, then sink into the grave,
Nor leave our broken hopes behind.

CONSTANCE.

Sнe sleeps, but as a marble saint
In some grand Gothic-windowed aisle,
When through rare glass the moonbeams faint
Upon her white face, seems to smile.

Thus sparkling o'er her sweet lips play
The joys of Love's immortal feast,
And on her glowing cheeks betray
Hues of a most delicious East.

Raise not thy lustrous eyes, my Love,
Those clear twin sapphires God hath wrought,
Nor speak, nor stir, but rest above,
In the calm sky of dreamy thought.

For who would wish with chain of earth

To check thy spirit's soaring flight,

Or quench one ray of heavenly birth

In the cold shade of sorrow's night?

ON THE DEATH OF COUNT CAVOUR.

AYE, mourning Italy, well mayst thou throw

Thy white arms o'er that well-beloved head,

Well may a rescued nation's voice of woe

Chant a grand requiem for the mighty dead,

And mourn their statesman's eagle spirit fled.

Who calmly cherished from his early youth,

With a far-sighted sense that Time shall prove,

A lofty dream of liberty and truth.

So that he loved his country with a love

Passing the love of women, for he laid

The might of a majestic intellect,

And tones that shook the senate, on her shrine,

High Thought that flew her falcon flight unchecked,

And keen wit piercing like a trenchant blade.

Such were his glorious gifts, our dead Cavour,

Now may they bloom beneath a light divine,

Because his aims were high, and conscience pure,

As theirs who thundered from the Aventine,

And seem to call from the far grave's long night,

' Again among the nations Rome shall shine

In the great glory of her People's right.'

CLIVE.

FAINT glanced the crescent through a cloud of shame,
O'er once proud trophies of the Imperial throne
Crumbling to dust, her waning lustre shone
Low in the Orient, when a Stranger came,
With lordship on his brow, and eyes aflame
With battle-yearnings, for the love of sway,
That thrilled his stormy boyhood's venturous play,
Through the man's heart was pulsing still the same.
Though haunting crime, that curse of high careers,
Saddened the bright eyes, set on Glory's goal
With over-earnest gaze, that brooked no peers,
Yet even above *your* war-drums' thundering roll,
Arcot and Plassey ! echoing through the years,
Sounds the deep voice of that victorious soul.

BENARES.

THY Gods have wrapt thee round as with a shroud,

Saintly Benares, where from morn till night,

From mosque-crowned street and temple-haunted
  height,

Throb out the voiceful murmurs of the crowd,

Over thy hallowed Ganges echoing loud;

While in the deep nook of each flower-clasped shrine,

Ever the speechless Shape, in calm divine,

Broods o'er the suppliant heads before him bowed.

But the majestic River rolls beneath,

Serene, relentless, bearing toward the sea

The dust of those, who, happy in their death,

By her blest margin meet Eternity.

Last, the clear sunset throws a golden wreath,

And the sweet Night sinks down most silently.

CAWNPORE.

The years roll on, the seasons wax and wane,
Since that great sorrow, when the craven crew
Round the doomed walls their traitor-legions drew,
And flashed the war-fires o'er the fatal plain.
Since that drear sunrise, when the toil-worn train
Sank down, death-smitten, in the waves of woe,
Happier than those who wept them, spared to know
The lingering horrors of the House of Pain.
O grief, that Time may soothe, but not make whole,
Thy one sad chord sounds true for evermore!
Yet not unblest the haunted waters roll,
For ever on the melancholy shore,
The star of God, the unconquerable soul,
Gleams through thy veil of darkness, dread Cawnpore!

HENRY LAWRENCE.

SOLDIER and statesman, whom the guiding star

Of Duty led serene from height to height,

For ever pure and stedfast for the right,

Through calms of peace, and thunder-clouds of war,

Still thy majestic name breathes hope afar

For us, who toil beneath the noonday sun,

But may not weary ere our work be done,

From the bright home where God's own chosen are.

Brave heart, who, when the Moslem's dread sur-

    prise

Leapt tiger-like upon us, dared be free

From human fears and passions, and arise

A tower of light upon a stormy sea,

A requiem, born of rescued Lucknow's sighs,

Floats o'er thy far-off grave eternally!

IN MEMORIAM.

Two sister empires chant the dirge of woe.

Not for the princely pageant, or the feast,

Meet in a warm embrace the West and East;

Fast fall their tears for CANNING's head laid low.

But when the voice of lamentation ceased,

I thought 'Though well may England mourn thy
      fate,

(She hath not many mightier men to show),

Great men, surviving glory, live too late.

So may our English nobles serve the State,

Like thy true heart, that, suffering, scorned to yield,

And, dying, taught our children to be great.

The man whose pure example almost shames

The Theban upon Mantinea's field,

Rienzi dying in the Roman flames.'

ON THE WRECK OF THE 'CHEDUBA.' *

NE'ER to be greeted on an earthly shore,

How swiftly, wafted deathward by the gale,

From the fair haven of their rest they sail

Into the silence, and are seen no more,

Nor shall be, till the waves give up their dead.

And we are left to weep and wail for these,

Clenched in the wild death-grapple of the seas,

And o'er their bones the surges rolling dread.

But let this trust among our tears have place,

That He, who walked the Galilæan wave,

Unveiled to them the glory of his face,

Whispering, 'The pure, the gentle, and the brave,

Shall sleep as calm within their storm-tost grave,

As in some English churchyard's green embrace.'

* This ill-fated steam-ship foundered in a cyclone which swept over the Bay of Bengal, in June, 1869.

ON THE HOOGHLY EPIDEMIC.*

In those lone hamlets, where the soft wind's breath
Laughs through the leaves on Ganges' palm-crowned
    bank,
But where the corpse-fed grass sprouts long and
    rank,
Heavily fall the silent shafts of death.
There the destroying Angel shakes his brand
Triumphant o'er the patient crowds, who lie
Pathetic in their voiceless agony,
And stalks relentless o'er the shuddering land.
Who wills a laurel o'er his brow to wave,
Greener than those of Plassey or Assaye ?

---

* For many years past a desolating fever has, from time to
time, ravaged the large and important district of Hooghly, in
Lower Bengal.

Let him close up the portals of the grave,

Thronged with that multitudinous array.

O Father! swift to smite, but strong to save

Thy children, let our ' strength be as our day ! '

THE CHAPTER OF THE STAR OF INDIA.

December 30, 1869.*

Our tranquil triumphs of to-day outbrave

The blood-besprinkled spoils of great Akbar,

And happier millions bless the milder Star

Of Her, who rules to cherish and to save ;

The sun of Hope illumines the Orient wave.

Let all dark deeds of kings and conquerors old,

And all our woes and warrings manifold,

Be hushed for ever in the silent grave.

The discords of the voiceful Past are laid,

Charmed by the might of music's golden sway,

In sleep, and as the stately cavalcade

Of Chiefs and Princes glows in bright array,

Ferozshuhr's lurid war-fires wane and fade,

Faint fall the far-off thunders of Assaye.

* The Duke of Edinburgh was invested with the insignia of a Knight of the Star of India at a special chapter of the Order, held with great splendour in Calcutta on December 30, 1869.

IN MEMORY OF JOHN PAXTON NORMAN.

An awful voice he heard, and might not stay

In that far city, where he grasped so long

The sword of Justice, temperate, calm, and strong.

Alas, the noble spirit past away !

'Tis not for us, frail creatures of a day,

To scan the Eternal purpose, or arraign

The sovereign Mercy, but not all in vain

We mourn the kindly voice, the genial sway ;

And mark the mellow wisdom, skilled to thread

The subtle web of wordy sophistries,

Melt into mild forgiveness, softly said

By dying lips, ere closed the dying eyes.

So muse I, while the Orient dews are shed

O'er the green turf where gentle NORMAN lies.

GALLE HARBOUR.

Lo, the sweet picture by God's hand wrought fair!

Here the all-golden summer lies asleep,

Hushed on the heaving bosom of the deep,

And kissed by snowy surges, rich and rare.

The havened trader through the noon-tide glare

Swings idly—like crowned queens amid the calm,

The tapering cocoa and her sister palm

Shoot high and happy in the affluent air.

Such scenes may soothe, not heal, the heart of man,

That aches with the old anguish still, nor know

Our souls the glorious gales Elysian,

(However soft our earth-born breezes blow),

Since through our Father's heart the death-thrill ran,

When our first Mother told him the first woe.

SEDAN.

THE Meuse runs red with slaughter, and we fall

Faster than leaves, by Autumn's whirlwinds blown ;

Our swords are shattered, and our hopes are flown,

And the white war-smoke veils with sulphurous pall

The death-throes of the German-vanquished Gaul.

But not in vain we perish ! not in vain

Fair France, our woe-worn Mother, clasps her slain,

While her hot tears drop heavily o'er all !

Better this hour of agony and shame

Than gilded fetters, and the Siren sway

Of Him whose strength was but a splendid name,

The visionary phantom of a day ;

For France must lead, not crouch, and free from

    blame

Of grasping falsehood, work her heavenward way.

A CHURCH IN SEDAN AFTER THE BATTLE.

THE day is o'er, the battle lost and won,

Fled the hot flush and fury of the fight,

The rushing squadrons and the charge of might,

The thunder-shouts of victory, all are gone.

But, whiter than the shapes of sculptured stone

That watch their slumbers, where the pale moon smiles

Through yon fair Church's angel-haunted aisles,

Can these be they by whom such deeds were done?

Raise, holy Priest, thy crucifix on high,

Sweet Sister, clasp the sufferers to thy breast,

Moisten the wan lips numb with agony,

And smooth their passage to the realms of rest,

Poor victims of a despot's fantasy.

How long shall these things vex us, God thrice-blest?

MACMAHON.

WARRIOR well-tried! though Fate has linked thy name
With that lost battle, and with France struck down,
Fear not the world's reproach, thy fair renown
Shines star-like through those mists of blood and
    shame.
Yet shall men greet thee with a proud acclaim,
As one who, mid the faithless faithful found,
When that death-volleying circle hemmed thee round,
Won from a falling cause immortal Fame.
Rest thou in peace, the future years shall bring
Triumphant solace for the praise grown cold;
War's laurels scarce are worth the gathering,
As the world ripens, and the years wax old.
But thou shalt smile, when calls the Eternal King
The victor and the vanquished, Chief high-souled!

'*AVE, CÆSAR IMPERATOR!*'

Is this the voice to bid our children bleed,

The Chief to sway the flaming brand of France,

To head the vanward of the world's advance?

Lo! we have leant upon a broken reed,

And found our golden idol clay indeed.

O brothers! *this* the Prince of peaceful years!

Nought shall we reap from him save blood and tears,

No brighter fruit can spring from such a seed.

His sun is setting in eternal gloom,

Nor even the warrior's glory gilds his pall:

Napoleon's self must smile within his tomb

At this mock Cæsar tottering toward his fall.

The Despot and the days are ripe for doom;

Who sees not God's handwriting on the wall?

NAPOLEON AT WILHELMSHÖHE.

SELF-SEEKING Shepherd of the innocent sheep,

Won to thy sway by fraud ! how just the doom,

That thou shalt sink inglorious to the tomb,

No laureled victors round thy grave to weep,

No patriot tears to sanctify thy sleep.

Yea, for thy Cæsar-forehead girt with bays

Of conquest, thou hast sown dishonoured days,

And nought save Dead-Sea fruit for France to reap.

Because no loftiness of thought endears

Thy visionary glory, based on crime,

O splendid Slave, not Conqueror, of the years !

We hail thy fall, most sad, but not sublime,

For thou hast missed his rich reward, who wears

The armour of pure Truth, unstained through Time.

PARIS.

DECEMBER, 1870.

How hath she fallen, that voluptuous Queen,
Whose splendid name was as a sword of might,
Dazzling the world with more than mortal light,
How hath she fallen from her height serene !
Lo, with her own lips hath she now to drink
The cup of trembling, while around her walls,
Yea, camped within her stately palace-halls,
The spoiler stands to smite, and will not shrink !
' Perish the nations, so that France's sod
Be sacred, France's soil inviolate.'
What steps are echoing where her kings have trod,
Where dead Napoleon sleeps in idle state ?
Most righteous judgment of a righteous God,
So perish all self-seekers, falsely great.

157

THE CAPTAIN.

WARRIORS unhappy! not for ye the crown
That wreathes their brows who fell at Trafalgar,
Flushed with the glories of victorious war,
And Nelson's name to sanctify renown.
But, while the great waves felt the Almighty's frown,
Rearing their foam-white crests against the sky,
And tossing their triumphant surge on high,
In the dread depths how horribly gone down!
What though our sorrowing country's love may
       make
Twin with the *victor*-souls, the hearts that *dare*,
Ere the bright eyes that weep, the breasts that ache,
Darkened and frozen by a deep despair,
Shall glow with hope, how many a morn shall break
On thy gray cliffs, storm-beaten Finisterre!

THE VICTORY.

DECEMBER, 1871.

I STAND upon the spot where Nelson fell,
Immortal in heroic agonies,
Victory glancing from his dying eyes,
And pale lips breathing that sublime farewell.
Upon me floats the deep o'er-mastering spell
Of the great sailor, and the day of fame,
When that last signal, flashing forth like flame,
Thrilled through our sea-kings o'er the ocean-swell.
O Ship of high renown, and ancient home
Of storied valour, to our hearts how dear!
For me thy memory-haunted planks become
Peopled with warriors, and again I hear
The proud three-decker plunging through the foam,
And the glad thunder of the victors' cheer.

THE NEOPHYTE.

By Doré.

FATHER of Mercies ! can it be for *this,*

I spurned the tranquil joys of social life,

And waging with thy gifts unhallowed strife,

Aimed fiercely at the mark I needs must miss ?

Lo, wildly striking out for realms of bliss,

I battle with the waves of agony,

And lost on an unfathomable sea,

Sink helpless in the horrible abyss !

No angel-voices break the deadly calm,

Wherefrom the wolfish faces on me glare,

Only the drear droned chant and death-cold psalm

Float o'er the rude white walls and benches bare.

Here must I pine and wither, as a palm

Planted amid chill blasts of Arctic air.

DARBOY.

Be this sublime death-lesson ne'er forgot,
But nerve us for high deeds—heroic pain.
Behold, he loved thy sons, who loved him not,
O fair sad city by the winding Seine!

To-day he heard the mighty organ-swell
Roll through his vast cathedral's holy calm,
To-morrow the deep gloom, the grated cell,
The scathing death-shot, and the martyr's palm.

He fell, but not where battle's bloody rain
Falls, blent with thunder of victorious cheers,
That soothe his sleep, who sinks amid the slain,
His country's triumph sounding in his ears.

'Twas his to pine in solitude, to wait
In awful silence, and sepulchral gloom
The last dread hour, when the grim prison-gate
Swung open, not for freedom, but for doom.

Such the dark death of him whom we deplore,
A bitter end, but calmly to be borne
By him, who from Life's ocean hailed the shore,
And spurned Time's sufferings with a lofty scorn.

And flashed no angel-arm to shield the just,
No thunderbolt of God?   Were this life all,
Curst were the hour that calls us from the dust,
Blest the drear sun that gilds our funeral-pall.

Gather the well loved ashes, in the glooms
Happy and hallowed lay him down to sleep,
Another beacon Time's sad path illumes,
Another watch-fire glitters o'er the deep.

M

THE POETS.

Not only o'er the realms of sea and earth,

But o'er the intellectual Day and Night,

The Poets reign by virtue of their might :

By music of sweet songs that have their birth

Fast by the fount of streams celestial,

Or by the force of trumpet-tones that call

From height to height, or grand prophetic strain

That takes the wings of morn, and will not die.

Thus are they guardians of the golden chain,

Whereby the unseen God in silence draws

Our throbbing world towards calm Eternity,

And shall be, while the endless ages roll.

For they are God's, those white-robed thoughts that

    pause

Upon the haunted threshold of the soul.

A PRAYER FULFILLED.

'FULL long the Olympian Zeus hath raged, full long

Lain heavy on his child his red right hand,

For lo ! with impious shout, and kindled brand,

The Persian stalks Athena's streets among.

There shall our fair Greek virgins dance no more,

Nor Pæans glad the victor-sons of song ?

Avenge us, mighty Father ! '   Thus the Greek,

While heaved the straining galleys off' the shore,

Arming for battle, breathed an ancient prayer,

Then, calmly dying, saw Themistocles

Rout the shamed Persians, leaving few to seek

Their own land o'er the blue Ægean seas,

While rent his royal robes, and tore his hair,

The great King on the Salaminian peak.

PINDAR.

THE wild swan wings her flight among the stars,

And Pindar soars above all other men,

Of snow-crowned steeps the mighty denizen,

Moving majestic o'er the golden bars

Of sunset to the halls where the Gods reign.

O for the joy of the proud charioteer,

Hot from the racing contest! when the bard

Swept the shrill chords and sung the victor strain,

Fresh as the lark's song from the dewy sward,

Pouring sweet praise on his delighted ear.

O thrice-blest king of happy Syracuse!

Crowned by the lofty Queen of lyric rhyme,

Who left for thee Parnassus' peak sublime,

And dipped her heavenly wings in earth-born hues.

RAPHAEL.

'In future generations who shall view

The King divine who bore the bitter rod ?

We soon shall die, who tread the paths He trod.'

Thus, while upon their hearts this sorrow grew,

Christ's servants breathed a sad prayer unto God.

So, when the time was ripe, a deep ray shone

O'er Raphael's artist-soul, the mastery

And music of the face that breathed upon

The rude waves of the Galilean sea,

And Jordan's sacred waters—till he knew

The patient face of Christ in dreams revealed,

And Mary by her Saviour Infant kissed,

The glorious Twelve, for heaven by sufferings scaled,

And Virgin saint, and loved Evangelist.

ON A PORTRAIT OF BEATRICE CENCI.

An everlasting love and agony
Immortal dwells in those calm earnest eyes.
Ah whence that gaze of passionate surmise ?
Some deep unfathomable mystery
Hath set a cloud upon that fair young brow,
As when black night sleeps on an Alpine peak.
On her pure neck her bright hair's golden glow
Streams calm as sunset, and from her pale lips
Deep thoughts and soft imaginations flow.
The bloom of youth hath faded from her cheek;
Fair lily, scathed too soon by Death's eclipse !
Yet seems she firm, and all too proud to weep.
Already in her heart the angels speak,
' 'Tis thus He giveth his beloved sleep.'

IN MEMORIAM E. B. B.

Not Britain only, but the land thrice blest,

Land of the hearts that burn, and songs that glow,

The land of Dante and of Angelo,

Wept, when the sceptred Sybil of the West,

Priestess of song, and stately Queen of thought,

Whose sunny strains might soothe an angel's rest,

When tired with toil for lost souls heavenward

    brought,

By Arno's banks lay in a last long sleep.

Whom stern Death clasping in a cold embrace,

Seized with a smile of triumph ere she died,

(Italian sunset falling on her face),

The silver sickle of her thoughts, that reap

The fleeting fruit of Fame from fields of space,

And left the world to mourn for light denied.

TURNER.

WHAT master-hand with freshening sunbeams dyed
Those mists o'er hill and valley rising far,
And hung upon the desolate mountain side,
Rose-red with stormy light, yon clouds of war ?
Who from yon rent crag hurled the avalanche ?
What tender and creation-loving heart
Hath showered a glory on yon withered branch ?
One whose deep night not Nature could illume,
The mightiest and most mournful Child of Art ;
Whose holiest thoughts are ever dashed with gloom.
Ye who would trace the source of human woes,
The worm i' the bud, the canker on the leaf,
Gaze awestruck on the golden hues of grief,
Where from the canvas Turner's genius glows.

MONTROSE.

My heart had burst to hear the cannon boom,

When the true Knight and stainless Cavalier,

Chief of the warrior-whirlwind of the North,

And pillar of the Stuart's falling throne,

Through crowds of traitors gallantly went forth,

(So sails a star through threatening clouds alone),

Drest for a wedding, to the place of doom.

Burns in the great heart of the mountaineer,

As long as Highland hills are crowned with snows,

For ever bright, the memory of Montrose,

The champion of our suffering Church and State.

Ah, not for silken ease such men are born,

Storm-beaten lives they live, defying Fate,

And dying, laugh the guilty world to scorn.

DUNDEE.

Stern Scottish soldier, loyal unto death,
Well may the Lowlands dread thine arm of might,
The warrior on the war-horse black as night,
Glorying to drink the battle's burning breath.
How like the Fiery Cross thy slogan flames
Over the rugged glen and wind-swept heath,
Where the wild clans are arming for King James:
Then the drooped head—the features wan with pain—
The death-pangs fanned by wings of Victory—
And the last look of beautiful disdain.
The mastery of thy name, thou great Dundee,
Stirs me, as if I stood in far-off lands,
And heard the first sound of an unknown sea
Break in the distance over desolate sands.

GARIBALDI AT SPEZZIA.

BECAUSE I knew thy soul was like the sea,

Spurning the shattered spoils of empty fame,

And not for statesman's crown, or splendid name,

Fought the good fight of Roman liberty,

I loved thee in that great triumphal hour,

When rang the death-shot on Magenta's heath,

And from her sleep roused startled Italy,

When France's legions hurled the Austrian power

From sulphurous Solferino's field of death;

Now that Fate's wave hath dashed thee from the

    prow,

And rude storms beat thy calm majestic face,

The shades of Roman chiefs shall crown thy brow:

Not the first Cæsar, dying at the base

Of Pompey's statue, seems more great than thou.

SERENADE.

As swiftly-glancing meteors in a dream
Play through a summer heaven the whole night long,
So on our souls immortal faces beam,
And one my heart hath moulded into song,
Fair as the minstrel-fabled shapes that throng
The haunted grove or music-hallowed fall.
Now let still Night uplift her starry pall,
Night, who alone can gentle thoughts inspire,
And my lone spirit, clasping all in all,
Chant a clear strain, and softly sound the lyre,
And breathe a low tune sweetly rising higher.
O, may no tears of sorrow e'er bedew
Those ever-glancing liquid orbs of fire,
Those ever-laughing eyes of heavenly hue.

MONTMORENCY FALLS.

O EVERLASTING avalanche of foam,

For ever hurrying onward, like the blast

That hurls his wintry wrath around thy home,

Through firs that frown like guardians of the past;

The bright waves on thy brow race fierce and fast,

Charmed by the voice of plunging surge below,

That lures them toward their white and ghastly

    grave

Of torture—their eternity of woe.—

So the three frenzied Sisters loved to rave

At sunset, on the far Sicilian shore,

Till the Greek seaman sought melodious death,

Maddened with wild strains yearning evermore.

O let me gaze on thee, and drink thy breath,

Thou glorious phantom crowned with ruin hoar.

IN MEMORY OF SIR JAMES OUTRAM.

OBIIT MARCH 11TH, 1863.

O DAY of darkness and of light,
O throbbing chords of joy and pain !
The bridal of a fair-haired Dane,
The death-hour of a noble Knight.

When blushing Love, in holy trust,
On happy hearts her signet placed,
Not far away Death's finger traced
' Ashes to ashes, dust to dust.'

When the rich-robed processions sweep
In solemn state up Windsor's aisle,
And rolling organs shake the pile,
Our Indian Bayard falls asleep.

While yet our hearts were all in flame,

Swift through our land Death's message past,

' Like him, be loyal to the last,

So shall ye mount through me to fame.'

So Death and Love their arms entwine,

And chant one grand funereal song,

' Uphold the right, war down the wrong,

And make the mortal more divine.

' Remembering him who kept his shield

Unsullied as the virgin snow,

Who never quailed before the foe,

Whose life was one great battle-field.

' Who, trained in Danger's sternest school,

Taught subject minds to view with awe

The majesty of England's law,

The glory of her Eastern rule.

' Who worked the purpose of his time,

From grasping love of self set free,

And crowned with great humility,

That only clings to souls sublime.

' Go forth, O song, with strength increased,

Far echoing from our English home,

O'er weary leagues of wild sea-foam,

And thrill the Princes of the East.

' That slothful men who lie reclined,

May rise, and heavenward set their feet,

And through the wakened earth may beat

The music of a noble mind.'

But we must mourn our son laid low,

From smiles to tears our spirits range,

And, with hushed voice and heart, we change

Our bridal-flowers for weeds of woe.

For him who spent his life to save
Our England in her hour of need,
The Faithful unto death, we lead
Another pageant—to the grave.

In state we keep, as best becomes
A chieftain sleeping after fight,
The burial of the tenderest Knight,
That ever heard the roll of drums.

With reverend hands we bear the pall,
Among our host of vanished stars,
O hero of our Indian wars,
Rest well within our Abbey wall.

IN MEMORY OF SIR HENRY DURAND.

ANOTHER light gone out on Glory's steep,
Another lofty chieftain sunk to rest,
Reft from our gaze, he sleeps his last long sleep,
In that fair land his ruling wisdom blest.

And we discern him, sanctified by death,
A soldier-statesman of heroic type,
Round whose grand brows fair gleamed the golden
     wreath,
Of mellow forethought, and experience ripe.

True to himself, his country, and his God,
Wearing high Thought's white armour, free from
     blame,
Through storms of war and toils of peace he trod,
With no uncertain steps, the ascent of Fame.

No sager counsel CHATHAM did unfold,

Than his grave utterance in the Hall of State,

No tenderer courage thrilled the knights of old,

Than fired the heart that glowed at GHUZNEE's gate.

So, when his praise waxed loud from shore to shore,

The long-tried champion of the public weal,

Well might his foemen in the days of yore,

Welcome the ruler worthy of their steel !

Peace to his memory, nor shall Time refuse

His place among the great in that proud land

Rich by his true life-service, nor the Muse

Grudge the green laurel to her own DURAND.

NATURE'S WARNING.

ALL sounds hushed, save the dreamy tune
That lulls the languid sleep of noon,
And sea and land are in a swoon.

A truce to grief, and guilt, and pain,
So ripe for harvest glows the plain,
So glad with white sails heaves the main.

But nature murmurs, 'Wherefore speak
Of Peace, when he who joy would seek,
Must breast the wave and climb the peak.

'Who scales that heavenly height shall feel,
Though age's frost his blood congeal,
His youth's first freshness o'er him steal.

' So sweet, so pure, so free from taint,

The glassed moon-beams that softly paint

The features of a dying saint.

' What first he suffers, only knows

The God who spread yon waste of snows,

Where every traveller comes and goes.

' For he must face the fiends of guilt,

Yea, though his heart's best blood be spilt,

With shield on arm, and hand on hilt.

'And he must tread the solitude

Of naked rocks, and deserts rude.

With wrecks of deep heart-yearnings strewed.

' And he must hear the wild winds blow

Songs of past joy and future woe,

The memories of long ago.'

Then I, with heart and brain on fire,
' What hope for those, who dare aspire
To grasp the glory of the lyre ?

' See Italy's majestic child,
Whose thoughts were Alps on Alps up-piled,
Move forth in tears, a man exiled.

' Mark him, who raised triumphal strains,
To sing the Cross's glorious gains,
His music might not break his chains.

' Hear Milton, whose ethereal mind
O'er time and space soared unconfined.
Chanting in darkness, old and blind.

' See him who raced with burning breath,
To pluck a faded laurel wreath,
Whom Famine darkly drove to death.

' See lofty Byron's towering flight,

Ideal majesty and might,

Sink into shades of endless night.

' The Genius of the subtle spell,

Who mourned so eloquently well,

I deem his verse Love's oracle ;

'Ah me, the wild waves' angry spray

Dashed o'er him rudely, while he lay

A drifting corpse in Spezzia bay.

' All these, who sang to harps of gold,

Have passed, with brows in shadows rolled,

Unto the land where all is cold.

' Far, far away, where none may list,

They mourn, by weeping Muses kissed,

But veiled in an eternal mist.'

Then Nature, ' He who meets his fate,
In faith, not downcast or elate,
Shall make his greatness trebly great.

' But he who builds an idle boast,
Above all men to shine the most,
What is he, but a wandering ghost?

' I own the lordly Florentine,
Though master of a Muse divine,
Far from his home was doomed to pine.

' Yet, trust me, he forgot his pain,
His wounded pride and high disdain,
When flashed the glory on his brain.

'And Tasso's soul shook off' the curse,
Weaving his long melodious verse,
For future ages to rehearse.

' Nor woe, nor chains, nor death can shame

The heavenly Bard's majestic fame,

Whose heart is pure and free from blame.

' But they who fly on wings of morn,

To depths of guilt, or heights of scorn,

Far better they had ne'er been born.

'What though the hearts of men may burn,

To mould the shrine, or chase the urn,

For souls who never may return ?

' The fame on which they place their trust,

The victor wreath, the marble bust,

Ends in a heap of empty dust.'

Thus Nature's language on me grew,

When night her starry mantle threw,

I, kneeling, felt her song was true.

o

THE OLD LOVE AND THE NEW.

Kiss me, I will not be refused,
Let me but feel the mystic token,
Or ever the silver cord be loosed,
Or ever the golden bowl be broken.
I ask you to love me, O my friend,
(Speak, for I die,) as the angels love
The prayers of a dying child, that blend
With the harmony born in heaven above.

Once was a time, when I well might deem,
That I to your heart could be all in all,
When the summer sunset's glorious gleam
Fell through the chink of the mouldering wall.
Calmly we talked near the castle old,
Of marriage joy in the years to be,

But the light in your eyes since that day grew cold,

And I knew that your love was not for me.

I know you noble and pure in heart,

Aye to a solemn purpose true;

Therefore I pray you, ere I depart,

Return me the love I bear to you.

I know you true to the sweet young life

We late saw laid in an early grave,

I know that the sacred name of wife

The soul from sin is mighty to save.

But the love that I seek from you is pure,

And as free from unfaith, or hint of blame,

As the winter stars, or the snows that endure

On Alpine mountains, ever the same.

To the home of your Love I travel to-night,

I am bound to the same far Spirit-land,

I shall meet her clothed in the robe of white,

And the secrets of earth we shall understand.

' Our Love,' I shall say, ' is left alone,

We have wandered from him through fields of air,

But ever before the golden throne

We both for his sake may breathe a prayer.

He is bound to us both by the chain that endears,

By love to you, and pity to me,'

And she will weep some angels' tears,

In spiritual sympathy.

Thanks, dear Love, for the pitying pledge,

On my ice-cold lips thus softly sealed ;

I had thought to blunt my sorrow's edge,

And die with my secret unrevealed.

Slowly your face from before me fades,

My body of earth to earth returning ;

But my soul can see through the grave's dark shades,

Where the starry lights of Heaven are burning.

www.ingramcontent.com/pod-product-compliance
Lightning Source LLC
Chambersburg PA
CBHW030545040726
47497CB00008B/2588